"You w

Garth stood in front of her hearth with the giant bowl of popcorn they had just made.

"Okaaaay. There are some in the little room." Lori headed in that direction. The request seemed a bit odd since he had never suggested a game before.

"I had something different in mind."

Her feet stopped in midstride, and she swung around to face him.

Garth's eyes were bright with delight. "Let's play 'I've got a secret.'"

Secret?

Her throat tightened, and her heart dropped to the pit of her stomach. Did he know? Of course not, how could he? But maybe he could sense she was holding something back, and this was his way to get her to come clean.

"It's easy. We take turns telling each other something about ourselves the other person doesn't know."

No, she wanted to shout. *Let's play something else—Boggle, Monopoly, Go Fish, anything else.*

"Come on. It'll be fun. We will learn interesting things about each other."

Fun?

"Please."

How could she get out of it without drawing attention to the fact that this honesty game scared her to death? "All right." How deep was this game supposed to be?

MARY DAVIS is a full-time writer whose first published novel was *Newlywed Games* from Multnomah. She enjoys going into schools and talking to kids about writing. Mary lives near Colorado's Rocky Mountains with her husband, three children, and six pets.

Books by Mary Davis

HEARTSONG PRESENTS
HP399—Cinda's Surprise
HP436—Marty's Ride
HP514—Roger's Return

Lakeside

Mary Davis

Heartsong Presents

Dedicated to my in-laws, Glenn and Joan,
whose lakeside cottage sparked the idea for this novel.

A note from the Author:
*I love to hear from my readers! You may correspond with
me by writing:*

**Mary Davis
Author Relations
PO Box 719
Uhrichsville, OH 44683**

ISBN 1-59310-607-6

LAKESIDE

*Our mission is to publish and distribute inspirational products offering
exceptional value and biblical encouragement to the masses.*

All of the characters and events in this book are fictitious. Any resem-
blance to actual persons, living or dead, or to actual events is purely
coincidental.

All scripture quotations, unless otherwise indicated, are taken from the
HOLY BIBLE, NEW INTERNATIONAL VERSION®. NIV®. Copyright © 1973,
1978, 1984 by International Bible Society. Used by permission of Zondervan
Publishing House. All rights reserved.

PRINTED IN THE U.S.A.

one

Lorelei Hayes slung a tote bag over her shoulder and grasped the handle of her suitcase before following her friend Josie into the cozy lakeside cottage. She smiled inwardly as she entered. It had been ten years, but the memories of that one special summer came flooding back to her. Good memories. The last of her good memories.

She dropped her bags in the bedroom she would call home for the next few weeks and headed for the sliding glass door that overlooked Starvation Lake.

Home.

One short, sweet summer and ten long, grueling years. Why did she feel as though she had come home?

Ten years. It seemed so much longer. A lifetime. She drew in a refreshing deep breath, and a peace washed over her. For the first time in years. *Home.* Odd. This had never been her home. In comparison she had spent so little time here. So much had happened since then. She had only been fifteen. Now she was a broken woman forced to make decisions at yet another crossroads in her life. She hated crossroads. They usually meant pain, both physical and emotional, as this one had.

As usual she chose to retreat for a while rather than move forward. She gave herself until the end of the year. She was entitled to at least that after the fire that swept through the house, not more than three months ago, took the only two people left in her life. The smoke still lingered in her nose and lungs—and mind. A dizziness invaded her head. She shook free the thoughts of the house ablaze and turned them back to the lake and that summer her life changed. She had found God here, or rather He had found her. She smiled.

She watched a motorboat race through the water with a

skier in tow. If she tried that now her hip would complain for a week. The boat motored past the peninsula and out of sight.

Her most vivid memory had to do with that peninsula the last day she had been here, almost ten years ago to the day at the end of August. She had swum out to the floating dock and stretched out in the sun. A small splash in the water next to the dock had caught her attention. Not really a splash, more like drips of water. She had turned toward the ladder as the dock tipped slightly in that direction. Over the side appeared a bronzed, lanky boy maybe two years older than she in red swim trunks.

His blond hair was slicked back. Water dripped from every part of him, puddling at his feet. He had run his golden hands over his face and hair to stop the water from streaming into his cornflower blue eyes as his gaze traced every feature of her face and her hair. She had sat mesmerized, gazing up at him. Who was this gorgeous hunk? And where had *he* been all summer?

After staring at her a moment, as if some internal debate had been going on, he made his move. He bent down and kissed her quickly on the lips. Before she could react, he turned with a grin and dove back into the water. She watched his sleek body glide along and disappear around the small peninsula.

She still didn't know who the boy was, but she had escaped back to this lakeside cottage in precious memories whenever she could. It added up to years spent here. Why? She had other happy memories before this place. But here God had touched her. And she hoped God would use this lakeside cottage to work miracles in her once again so she could turn this new corner in her life and move on. This was where she would fight for the will to go on, for something to want to live for. Her future.

In her head she could hear the echo of Doug's insistent voice. "What's your praise for the day?"

She had no praises and nothing left for which to be thankful.

"Come on—think of a praise."

Doug would keep after her until she ground out some word of thanks, some praise. But she had no family left. All her loved ones were dead. She had no home and no direction for her life. All she had was more insurance money, and she was not thankful for that.

"Just one praise."

She hadn't come up with a single praise since the fire. Her life seemed so empty. She had nothing left—except God. *God, I praise You for—for being God.* That was the best she could do. A familiar peace wrapped around her like a gentle hug. *Thank You for not abandoning me.*

She sighed with relief. It had been too long since she'd last acknowledged God. A smile pulled at her mouth.

A knock on the front door brought Lori back to the present. Josie hurried to answer it. "Hi, Shawn!"

"Hey, Josie. How are ya doing?"

"Fine. Come in—come in." Josie stepped aside to let an attractive blond man enter. "It's good to see you."

He wore a blue golf shirt and khaki shorts, and his features reminded her of a Viking. "I won't stay long. I know you have to unpack, open up the place, and turn everything on; but when I saw the car pull in and you get out, I had to rush right over. A lot of the old gang are up here this weekend. We're having a fire on the beach over at my place tonight. The last fire of the summer."

"Who?" Josie asked. "Is Anna here?"

His smile broadened as he nodded. "And Rich, Melinda, and, of course, Garth, but he's always here."

"What about Ryan and—Audrey and the rest of the Kessels?" Josie said with a wave of her hand.

"No, just Garth. I think Ryan started back to school already. Med school must be tough."

They prattled on about various others Lori knew nothing about and had no interest in. They would have the fortune of a normal memory and might remember her, but she wouldn't have a clue about them. Her memory wasn't what it used to be since the accident. Like pumice, full of holes.

"Yeah. Well, can we expect you two tonight?" The Viking warrior threw a glance and a dashing smile in Lori's direction.

"How rude of me. Shawn, this is my friend Lori. She spent a summer up here with me one year. You probably met her then."

Shawn and Lori stepped forward and gave each other a cordial handshake. His hand felt warm and strong in hers. He held it a moment longer than necessary.

"Lori, this is Shawn Hill. They have the place two doors down. You want to go tonight?" Josie sounded eager.

The morbid cloud that had hung over her the last ten years weighed heavier now without Doug. She didn't feel like pasting on a smile and being around a bunch of strangers. "I don't mind if you go."

"I'm not going without you," Josie said to her with compassion in her eyes then turned back to Shawn. "We may or may not make it."

The blond stepped outside as Josie held the door open. "Everyone will be disappointed not to see you," he said.

"I'll talk her into it," Josie said in a conspiratorial whisper.

"We're gathering around eight, and we'll start the fire after nine when the wind changes."

Josie closed the door.

Lori watched as her friend turned her sad brown eyes and pouty lips on her. What defense did she have for that? Could she deny Josie a reunion with her friends? Besides, just because she went didn't mean she had to stay. "What does one wear to a campfire?"

⁊⁏

Lori stood on the outskirts of the group of happy, chattering people. Josie had introduced her all around and was now catching up with her friends, but Lori didn't know any of these people. At least she didn't think she knew them.

Shawn, however, seemed to take it as his personal responsibility to see she was not left out. He made sure she had a soda and wasn't ignored. His thoughtfulness was starting to wear on her. He was a tall, handsome man with a firm, square jaw and almost transparent blue eyes. All he needed was the proper clothes, a helmet with horns and a sword, and he could plunder the Scandinavian seas.

If it were another time in her life, she would probably like the attention, but being social was not on her agenda for anytime in the near future. Maybe when they lit the fire she could fade into the shadows and slip away. She didn't want to stay for the fire anyway. She didn't like fire.

"When do you start the fire?" She could do her part at polite conversation. And it would let her know when she could plan her escape.

"After nine," he said with a glance at his watch. "Twenty to thirty minutes more."

Ten minutes later Shawn excused himself from her side to greet a latecomer. He, too, was tall and handsome, standing well over six feet, but his blond hair was a few shades darker than Shawn's, not quite a sandy color, much richer looking. He had on a button-up blue plaid shirt with matching solid blue pants. He looked as if he'd just stepped off the cover of a magazine. Perfectly put together.

Something was familiar about him, but she couldn't put her finger on it. Had she met him before? Why did none of the others seem familiar? But then pumice was like that. Maybe, because of his good looks, she wished she remembered him and then would have common ground to hold an intelligent conversation.

That's when she noticed the beautiful blond next to him. Her long silky hair draped over her shoulder in a mass of loopy curls. He had a girlfriend. Or wife.

Oh, well. She reminded herself she wasn't sociable these days anyway.

Shawn and the other blond man retreated into the cottage

with the bag he was carrying.

Her chance had come, alone at the edge of the group. No one was paying any attention to her. No one would notice if she disappeared into the night. Josie would understand. She glanced one last time at the door, which the new man had passed through with Shawn. What was so naggingly familiar about him?

Forcing memories that lingered below the surface had always proved futile, so she had given up on remembering anything from her past that didn't jump into her head of its own accord. When she did remember something from before the accident, before the pain, she wrote it down, afraid of losing what little she had collected of her past.

She would give up on remembering this man, if indeed she had anything to remember. It had been a very long time since she had snagged a new piece of her history. She pushed it all aside and turned to leave.

"Hi. I'm Gretchen Kessel. I don't think we've met," said the blond girl who had arrived with the mystery hunk. Her smile appeared genuine.

Lori found herself shaking Gretchen's outstretched hand, and soon they were talking like old friends. Gretchen was warm and inviting and seemed truly interested in Lori. As much as Lori wanted to dislike her, she couldn't. So friendly and personable—and perky.

"You have to meet Bash." Gretchen pointed to the gorgeous man she'd arrived with.

What had Gretchen called him? Bash? What kind of name was that?

Before Lori could protest, Gretchen took her by the hand and led her over to him.

"I'll catch you later," said a dark-haired man who was talking to this Bash. "I'm going to help Shawn and the others with the fire."

"If they need someone who knows what he's doing—," the blond man started to say.

"I know. I know." The dark-haired man raised his hand. "We'll give you a holler, Mr. Expert Fire-Builder."

"Hey, Happy. I see you made a new friend," Bash said to Gretchen then turned his gaze on Lori.

Happy? It fit her.

"Garth, this is my new friend Lorelei Hayes," Gretchen said.

In that instant, when his deep blue eyes settled on her, the image of a Garth ten years younger flashed before her, tall and lanky, dripping wet. He had changed considerably since then. He had filled out, and his hair had darkened from bleached blond to a honey gold. But she recognized his eyes. Those captivating blue eyes had studied her face for a moment ten years ago before—before he kissed her and dove into obscurity. She felt her cheeks warm slightly at the memory. Good thing it was nearly dark.

"Lorelei," Gretchen said, bringing her back to the present, "this is my big brother Garth Kessel. Well, one of my big brothers." Garth gave her a quick nod as Gretchen went on. "He's a science teacher at the high school in Kalkaska."

Garth Kessel, she repeated to herself. *I always wondered what your name was. Brother?* That had a nice sound to it.

"Lorelei's staying at the Davenports'," Gretchen continued, unaware of the mental trip Lori was taking. "She's staying for a few weeks, maybe even a couple of months, while she recovers from a death in the family. She sold her place down in Florida and came up here for a while."

How did she do it? How did Gretchen get so much information out of her in a short time? Hadn't Gretchen done most of the talking? Evidently not.

"You have a pen, Bash? I think I have a gum wrapper somewhere." The two went fishing in their pockets and came up with a pen and gum wrapper at the same time. Gretchen took the pen as she continued to tell Garth all she had learned about Lori. She put the scrap of paper on her raised knee and wrote as she talked without hesitation. Silently Garth held her arm to steady her. He never tried to interrupt her or quiet her. He just let her rattle on and on.

"Here." She handed the paper to Lori. "If you need any-thing, anything at all, just give Garth a call. He's a whiz at fixing things, can fix just about anything. He's gone during the day at school—I told you he's a teacher, didn't I? Yeah, I did. Well, he's home most evenings and weekends. And if he's not there, just leave a message on the machine."

She turned to Garth, thrusting the pen back at him. "You don't mind, do you, bro? Lori's going to be alone up here."

Garth smiled with a slight shrug. "Call me big brother to the world."

"He is so great, the best," Gretchen said to Lori. "Can you believe no one has snatched him up yet? He doesn't even have a girlfriend. I can't imagine any woman letting him go. He's a great guy."

Garth rolled his eyes.

"Who is that with Anna?" Gretchen said. "Do you know, Bash?"

"Can't say that I do," Garth said, unaffected by the sudden change in topics.

"Someone new to meet. A friend to make." Gretchen turned back to Lori. "It was great meeting you. I'm sure I'll talk to you again before the night is over. See you later."

Lori stared after the delightful young woman, watching her blond curls bounce as she went.

Garth chuckled. "She has that effect on people."

Lori looked up at him. "Huh?"

"Gretchen. She tends to leave you speechless."

"Is she always so—" Lori searched for a word that wouldn't sound critical, for she really liked her.

"Energetic?" Garth offered. Lori nodded. "Pretty much. She's up a few notches from normal. She gets that way when she's upset."

"Upset?"

His smile slipped away. "She just broke up with her boyfriend."

Lori shook her head. "I never would have guessed."

"Gretchen thrives on people. She copes with hurt and stress best when she's in a crowd. Only when she is content and happy can she handle being alone for very long. Sometimes it gets her down to be alone. People energize her. When she's worked through her initial hurt, she'll sort things out."

His concern for his sister touched her in a place deep inside she thought was dead. "Not me. I like being by myself. That's why I came up here."

"Solitude has its rewards."

His steady gaze unnerved her. She fingered the wrapper unconsciously in her hand. "Oh. Here." She held the paper out to him. "You probably want this back."

"Keep it." He raised his hand like a traffic cop to stop her. "Gretchen didn't speak out of turn when she offered my help. She knows I'd be more than happy to do what I can. If you need anything or have any questions, please feel free to call on me. Sometimes things break at inopportune times."

"Thanks." She slipped it into her pocket, knowing she would not use it. But what else could she do not to offend him?

A moment of uncomfortable silence stretched between them. She had been eager for the fire to be lit so she could slip away, but now she wasn't so sure. "Why do they wait until after nine to start the fire?"

"During the day the breeze blows from the lake up to the cottages. Around nine or so the breeze blows out toward the lake, taking the smoke from the fire with it, keeping the inside of the cottages from smelling like smoke." He looked comfortable.

She, on the other hand, had to concentrate on controlling her fickle emotions. She had desperately wanted to leave. Now she found that idea less appealing. "Does the wind do that every night?"

"Pretty much."

"Why?"

He wiggled his eyebrows up and down and with a glint of

mischief in his eyes said, "It's magic."

She smiled. It had been a long time since her mouth had turned in an upward direction. It felt refreshing. "I don't think so."

"It's true. The fluttering of thousands of fairy wings causes the breeze. They're invisible, of course, and live in the trees." Merriment danced in his words, as well as in his eyes. "After sunset they come out to gather water once the fish have gone to sleep. If they gather water during the day, the fish see their shadows and try to eat them." He made a jaw-snapping motion with his hand.

"I thought they were invisible."

"Not entirely. That's why the fish can see their shadows dancing on the water. If you look carefully, every once in a while you can see a ripple in the breeze as a fairy passes by." He shook his head as he looked at her. She had an eyebrow arched in disbelief. "You aren't buying any of this, are you?"

"I don't believe in fairies, and I don't believe in magic." *In fact, I don't believe in much of anything these days.* "You want to try again?" She found she wanted to keep him talking to hear his smooth voice wash over her. She wanted to pretend he cared for her and wasn't just being polite in keeping her company.

"Gretchen never believed that story either. Actually, after the sun goes down, the air cooling combined with the warm lake water causes the shift in the air."

"Why's that?"

With her interest piqued he switched into what Lori could only describe as "the teacher mode" and gave an in-depth, scientific explanation of how and why air travels. He didn't talk down to her but explained everything so she could understand it.

After "the lesson" they gathered around the fire with the others, roasting hot dogs and marshmallows and making s'mores. She guessed some of the food items were in the bag he was toting when he arrived.

"Do you remember the three summers of the bandit?" a guy closest to the fire asked.

"You mean the kissing bandit," one woman said, and all the women giggled.

"Craig claimed to be the bandit, but I'm sure he wasn't."

"Several guys tried to claim the title."

The discussion bounced back and forth across the fire. The women reverted to schoolgirls as they reminisced. The men seemed envious of the bandit and puffed up their chests.

"It was a guy from the other end of the lake."

"Didn't Justin Edward live down that way?"

"A lot of people thought he was the one."

"Josie, didn't you fall victim to the kissing bandit?"

"Who didn't? Between the three summers of his escapades I don't think anyone escaped unkissed."

Lori's mouth went dry, very aware of the blond "bandit" next to her. Had he really kissed Josie and the others? He didn't seem the type. At least she hoped not. Should she blow his cool cover and tell them she knew who he was?

"Some were kissed more than others," one girl said, eyeing another.

"How many times?" someone coaxed.

She shyly held up five fingers on one hand and three on the other.

"Eight?"

"All that first summer," her friend said.

"Anna, didn't you date Justin one summer? Was it him?"

"Wellll," she said with a knowing smile.

"She knows; she knows!"

"Spill the beans. We want to know everything."

"It was Justin that first summer. But the next summer when we started going out I made him hang up his cape and mask."

Cape? Mask? Lori didn't remember any cape or mask. But then he had made a water assault. Extra clothing probably would have weighed him down.

Anna went on. "His cousin, Wayne, took up the mission in his place. They look a lot alike, same brown hair, brown eyes, similar build."

That's not what my bandit looked like. Lori, lost in her thoughts, momentarily left the group and the fire far behind. *No cape or mask, and his eyes were most definitely a marvelous shade of blue.*

She stole a quick sideways glance at the man next to her. He seemed unaffected and bored by the whole silly conversation, staring into the fire. Did he even remember a red-haired fifteen-year-old girl sitting on the floating dock? She supposed it didn't matter if he did or not. Her memory was probably playing tricks on her anyway, piecing together unrelated details to come up with a wild and intoxicating tale.

"I wonder why Justin thought to do it in the first place," someone asked, pulling Lori's wayward thoughts back to the fire.

Anna's friend piped up again. "Because he was too afraid Anna would turn him down if he asked her out. He thought jumping out of the bushes, scaring everyone half to death, was more effective."

Laughter erupted around the fire.

Lori stole another quick glance at her own personal bandit. *And why did you do it?*

two

Brother and sister walked side by side in a companionable silence along the beach, heading toward home. The moon was high, and the stars twinkled brightly.

As they passed the Davenports' place, Garth gave a pensive glance at the cottage cloaked in darkness, inside and out. Josie and Lorelei had left the gathering early, more than an hour and a half ago. Both women claimed fatigue from the long drive up, and Josie had to make the return trip tomorrow; but her friend with the silky red hair and bright green eyes would be staying. His lips curved up slightly at the corners.

"Thank you, Garth."

Gretchen's soft, sad voice brought his thoughts back to his hurting sister at his side. "For what?"

"For being you." She was more somber now than earlier. "You never push. You wait, and I know you'll be there when I need you. You let me be me and work through things my own way. You're a good listener. And a good friend."

"I'm glad you know you can come to me." He put his arm across her shoulder and gave her a little squeeze.

"I'm glad, too. You're a lot like Mom, you know?"

"Thanks. I take that as a compliment."

She looked up at him in earnest. "It was meant as one."

After a moment of silence he knew she wasn't ready to talk about the real problem yet. "Are you in a hurry to leave in the morning, or will you come to church with me?"

She gave a graceful wave of her hand and said in a stately tone, "I would be most honored to be escorted to church by my handsome bachelor brother.

"Bachelor," she repeated in normal tones. She looked at

17

him with the same thoughtfulness in her eyes that was in her voice. "It doesn't suit you, Bash. I don't think you were meant to be alone your whole life."

He shrugged. "It's worked so far."

"You've never been one to date much, a casual date here and there with a friend or colleague but nothing remotely serious. It's as if your heart has been waiting for Miss Right and will settle for nothing less."

"Is that so?" He unlocked the door to his cottage. It was actually the family's, but he called it home.

"Yes. I know you too well, Mr. I'm-Just-Fine-As-I-Am. Tonight I'll start praying for a wife for you." She smiled and slipped inside.

"Anyone in particular?" If his sister was going to start playing matchmaker as others had tried, he wanted to know who would be thrust his way. It seemed everyone had a daughter, sister, cousin, niece, or friend who would be perfect for him.

"I can think of a few possibilities off the top of my head."

A few! He raised his eyebrow. "Anyone I know?"

"Some maybe, some maybe not," she said with a flourish and escaped into her room before he could question her further.

He hated it when people tried to set him up with someone. Well-intentioned friends and family were not welcome in this matter. But his little sister was right on one account; he was not meant to be a bachelor his whole life—for now, yes, but not forever. He hoped his future included a wife and children.

He viewed himself as belonging to the one God had chosen and tried to act in a way befitting an engaged man. He didn't want his fiancée to be presented to him while he was dating someone else just to pass the time. God had someone special for him—in His time.

Soon, he hoped.

He would also pray tonight. Pray his sister would become

so involved in her studies she would forget about meddling in this single brother's life.

❧

A light far off in the distance came closer and closer.

It was coming for her again.

There was no escape.

Brighter and brighter.

Not a single light but a pair of lights.

Headlights barreled down on her. She tried to scream, but it was too late.

She always tried to scream.

She couldn't breathe. Something pressing on her chest prevented her from grasping a normal breath.

Shooting pain accosted her head. Reaching up, she touched the throbbing that intensified with each breath. It came back wet. . .thick. . .like cherry-pie filling. Her white sweater would be ruined.

Tired. . .so tired. . .and cold. The scene faded as she thought of her parents in the front of the car. She could hear no sound from them. Darkness closed in around her, and she knew she was slipping closer to death. It neither scared nor comforted her. It simply was. The darkness enveloped her, and she sank into its waiting arms.

Then suddenly she was wandering in the middle of the road with a young orphaned child in her arms. She held the crying child close and rocked it.

Without warning the child was wrenched from her arms.

She cried out for the child.

What little light there was faded.

Darkness blanketed her.

Alone.

Invisible walls closed in on her—pressing—suffocating.

Smoke.

She couldn't breathe again.

So much smoke.

Lori woke, gasping for air.

"Doug," she cried softly into the night.

Always the same dream. The two worst days of her life woven into one.

≥

Lori stood with her arms wrapped around herself, staring out the large picture window at the small lake, remembering a better time. She loved it at this place.

Josie's parents used to spend the entire summer at their cottage, and weekends and holidays during the rest of the year as Josie grew up. Now they were too busy to spend much time at all up here. They were more than happy to say yes when Josie asked if her old friend could use it. Josie was so lucky to have a lakeside cottage retreat at her disposal.

Lori would like to have a cozy place like this. She had plenty of insurance money to buy one or a dozen—the whole lake if she wanted. She would rather have Doug and Aunt Lillah back—and her parents. If she were wishing, she might as well wish for them all.

That night ten years ago still caused an ache deep down, the outcome devastating. The pain of a more recent night haunted her day and night. She pushed the agonizing memories aside as a single tear slid down her cheek.

"Are you sure you want to be up here alone?" Josie came up beside her and draped her arm around her shoulders. "I could try to get some time off and stay."

Lori wiped the tear away. "Jos, I'll be fine. I need some time to myself, to think."

"Okay, but just don't isolate yourself."

A bit of isolation was exactly what she needed. "I just need to figure out what God's purpose is in all of this."

Loneliness enfolded her as her friend left, but at the same time she longed for the solitude. Time to think and cry, to figure out what was in store for her for the future and what she was going to do with her empty life.

≥

Garth straddled the bench-press seat and lay back under

the bar. The all-in-one weight machine afforded him the freedom to work out in his own private gym down here in the cool basement whenever he wanted. During the school year he liked to work out on the school's equipment. It gave him a chance to connect with some of the students. He gripped the metal rod with both hands and took a deep breath.

She's here! After all these years she's finally here. He had made the right decision to teach in northern Michigan. He pressed up on the bar and did twelve repetitions in fast succession. Not only was she here, but she was also as wonderful as he imagined. No, more so. He did twelve more rapid presses. Or was it thirteen?

Those green, green eyes gazed up at him in disbelief as he told her the fairy story. He didn't know what possessed him to tell it, but he was glad he did. The look on her face was priceless. He would savor it for a long time.

His last set of twelve went slower, but he still wasn't breathing heavily. Had someone changed the weights on him? No, it was his usual 290. It must be the added energy he had today.

Moving on to lateral pull-downs, leg lifts, leg extensions, and leg curls, he worked out quickly and eventually broke a sweat. As he did he formulated a plan to talk to the red-haired beauty again then ask her out.

When he was finished, he leaned back against his weight machine with a crooked grin. She still held onto her youthful looks with the exception of her shorter hair. That's what had caught his attention originally, all that red hair, spilling down her back, glistening in the sun.

He jumped up when the phone rang and bumped his head on the bar above him. *Lorelei!* He dove across the room to answer before the machine upstairs picked up. If she reached the recording, she might not leave a message.

"Hello!"

"Hi, honey."

His enthusiasm dipped. "Oh, hi, Mom." He held his palm on the rising lump on his head. Why should it be Lorelei? Just because Gretchen had forced his phone number on her and he wanted it to be her.

"I'm sorry to disappoint you, son."

He picked up the cradle of the slim-line phone and walked back over to the weight machine to snatch his towel. "What's up?" He wiped the sweat from his face and draped the towel around his neck.

Should he tell his mom about Lorelei? That the girl he hadn't been able to get out of his head for the past ten years had come back to him? Well, not to him but to Starvation Lake. That she was wonderful and sweet and had the most gorgeous red hair he had ever seen?

"Is she pretty?"

"Oh, yes." He realized what he'd said and snapped out of his daydream. "What? No! What do you mean?"

"Garth, I'm your mother," she said in a no-nonsense tone. "If you don't want to talk about her, that's your business."

He slumped down on the couch and sighed heavily. "Very pretty."

"Do you want to tell me about her?"

"She's a red-haired angel with a cute little nose sprinkled with freckles."

"Does she have a name?"

"Lorelei." He let her name linger on his tongue. "Isn't that a beautiful name?"

"It sounds as if her name could be Mud and you'd still think it was beautiful."

"Huh? What?"

"Nothing, son," she said with a smile in her voice. "Have you two been seeing a lot of each other?"

"Shawn Hill had a beach fire last night. She was there."

"You've only seen her once?"

"Not exactly." He shifted on the couch and sat forward, resting his forearms on his thighs. "You remember when you and Dad first bought this cottage? We spent the last two weeks of summer up here?"

"I remember."

"Josie Davenport had a friend visiting with her for the summer."

"This woman who has captured your heart after one meeting is the same girl you snuck over and kissed when you were a boy?"

He sat up straight. "You knew about that?"

"You were glued to one tree at the edge of our property for two weeks. How could I not know? I worried about you. Suddenly you were gone. I saw you steal that kiss."

"I didn't know what to say to her."

"Hello would have been nice."

Yeah, if my brain had been working. He wiped the fringes of his face and along his jaw with the towel.

"Did you do better this time around, or did you just grab her and kiss her again?"

He wouldn't dignify his mom's poor joke with an answer. But he did wonder what it would be like to kiss Lorelei again one day. "I talked her ear off. I hope I didn't bore her with my scientific mumbo-jumbo." He took a deep breath and leaned back on the couch. "She has a nice smile." He pictured her smiling at him as he spun his fairy tale. "A gentle, welcoming smile. Do you think I should have told her it was me ten years ago?"

"Absolutely not. If she remembers—"

"I don't think she does. She didn't recognize me." He would have cringed inwardly if she had. He couldn't believe when the conversation wandered around to the bandit. If she were going to remember, it would have been then.

"*If she remembers,*" his mother said firmly, "it will only embarrass her and put your relationship on an awkward footing. And if she doesn't, your feelings won't be hurt for not making a lasting impression."

"You're probably right." His mother had insight and a

woman's instinct. Her advice had always been good.

After a moment of silence his mother said, "When are you going to see her again?"

He could hear the hope in her voice. "I was thinking of going over later in the week and inviting her to church with me on Sunday." A crick was forming in his neck, so he switched the phone to his other ear and rotated his head to loosen his neck.

"That sounds good; then you can find out where she stands spiritually."

"I'm sure she's a Christian." She had to be. He cradled the phone with his shoulder and picked at a loose thread on the arm of the aging green sofa bed.

"Just because you wish it doesn't make it so."

"She has to be a Christian. Josie's a Christian." The three-inch strand pulled free. He wound the couch fiber around his little finger then unwrapped it and did it again. He was wrapped around Lorelei's finger, and she didn't even know it.

"I hope so. I'll keep you both in my prayers. I really called to see how you were doing. I hadn't talked to you in a while. Since it seems you're doing great, I won't keep you any longer; I'm sure you still have a lot of preparing for school."

"A boatload."

"Keep your mind on your task, and you'll get through it."

"Easier said than done." He rolled the thread up into a ball and let it drop to the floor. The green shag carpet swallowed it immediately.

"I know. I look forward to hearing more about your Lorelei. And meeting her?"

Garth smiled. "That's the plan."

He could imagine his mom singing the "Hallelujah Chorus" in her pause.

"I love you, son."

"Love you, too. Give Dad my love."

Garth hung up the phone and leaned back on the couch. His mother raised a question he had not thought of. What if Lorelei wasn't a Christian? It troubled him to consider it, but after a moment he jumped to his feet. "Then I will have the honor and privilege of introducing her to the Lord."

I wonder what she's doing right now. Lord, whatever she is doing, please be with her and soften her heart toward You if she doesn't know You. And if she does know You, soften her heart toward me.

The sun was low in the sky, casting long shadows, when he stepped outside. The water lapped gently against the shore. He drank in the heady scent of the pines and the less potent poplars. He turned toward the Davenports' property. Surprised to see Lorelei sitting at the picnic table on the beach, he ducked behind a familiar tree. He felt seventeen again. He looked around the tree. She seemed so delicate in her white blouse and floral print skirt. The setting sun set her hair ablaze as she wrote in a spiral notebook.

Miss Lorelei Hayes, are you merely a vision I conjured up from years of longing? Or are you real?

The breeze that rippled her shirt blew a strand of her shoulder-length hair across her face. Her pen continued to scratch on the page. He wanted to brush the errant strand back for her. Not until she finished did she remove the lock from her face. She closed her notebook and stood slowly. Rubbing her right hip, she looked around, her gaze headed in his direction. He ducked behind the tree and held his breath. He *was* seventeen again and a sorry case, at that. After a moment he ventured a peek.

She struggled up the incline to the cottage with her notebook under one arm and a hand cradling her hip. Was that a slight limp he detected? Probably stiff from sitting on the hard bench. He could relate.

"Good-bye, Lorelei. I'll see you in a few days."

three

On Monday Lori sat at the large oak table, turning her now-empty mug around and around.

Garth Kessel.

The man's name as well as his face drifted in and out of her thoughts. She couldn't shake him. It was a nice name. She liked it. It fit him. His strong jawline on his slightly baby face. But his eyes. She had to force herself not to look at his eyes for fear of being sucked into their blue depths with no idea of what he was saying.

She shook her head. Just the thought of them drew her in. Perhaps a walk would clear her mind of him. She trotted off to the bedroom and slipped on her white canvas sneakers then tucked her keys into her pocket. Out the door and up the hill to the road.

At the top of the driveway she stopped. Left or right? Left went down to the little store and gas station on the corner. She wanted a longer walk than that, so she turned right and started the three-mile hike around the lake. She had done it many times the summer she visited up here, and Josie had refreshed her memory on how easy it was.

The poplars and the maples rustled in the breeze. Not far up the dirt road a wooden sign caught her attention, and she stopped. *The Kessels.* Her heartbeat quickened. Like most of the people who had summer cottages up here, the Kessels had their territory staked out. Gretchen had told her it was her parents' place, but Garth had taken it over year-round. She didn't realize he lived so close. She strained to look down the long, grassy driveway with tire trails. That was the cottage with the small peninsula. Shadows blanketed the building below, obscuring her view. He wasn't

26

there, of course; he was at work.

A car kicking up dust on the rutted road startled her and quickly put her legs in motion. She let out a puff of captive air when she realized the vehicle was not turning down the Kessel drive and it was not Garth.

That was close.

What if he had been coming home after a forgotten lunch bag or students' papers and caught her snooping around his place? She stepped around a flattened snake in the dirt and picked up her pace to put some distance between her and the Kessel place.

Why do I keep thinking about that man? I try so hard to think of anything and everything except him. But, to no avail, my thoughts return to him.

Was it because his was the face she had clung to when the physical pain got to be too much after the accident? Or could it be the mystery and romance of that kiss so long ago? But now that the mystery was solved, shouldn't she be able to forget him? Had he become so much a part of her thoughts that he was a permanent fixture? Was there anything that would dispel him from her brain? Did she want that to happen?

With so many confusing thoughts bombarding her, she longed to be back at the cottage with her journal. She could sort things out so much better if she could write them down and see them.

One good thing that had come from her preoccupation with Garth Kessel was not thinking about the fire and the double funeral. She wasn't wallowing in her grief. She looked forward to each new day. In hopes of seeing Garth Kessel? No, it couldn't be. But she had to admit, she couldn't remember the last time she didn't have to work hard to climb out of bed in the morning. It was probably the fresh northern Michigan air that stirred the life back into her.

She did have a nagging feeling of some unfinished business with the man. What could it be? She had met him twice and only talked to him once. What dealing could she have with him?

Was she supposed to tell him she knew who he was? Not in a million years!

Three quarters of the way around the lake, she put her hand to her right hip. "I know—I know—I haven't forgotten you're there." The pain wasn't enough to inhibit her walk yet—just enough to remind her she was the sole survivor of a deadly accident and her life would never be the same.

She'd heard that people with head trauma, especially as severe as hers, usually had no memory of the accident. Why was she stricken with every last detail of the horrific event? Her mother's scream. The car rolling. The searing pain. The blood. The deadly silence. The utter darkness.

She wished she had lost her memory entirely, except one that involved a certain blond-haired blue-eyed bandit and a floating dock. She smiled. Yes, she always wanted to remember Garth.

She'd had a long road of countless surgeries and hours of therapy to regain what function she could of her body. A journey, if given the choice, she would not have made.

She never really said good-bye to her parents. The fact she was comatose and hooked up to external plumbing seemed to warrant the doctors' keeping her from attending her parents' funeral. Then she was whisked away to Florida to her only adult living relative to finish her recovery. No wonder she felt compelled to come back to Michigan to say her final farewell at their graves. At last she was closing that chapter of her life.

But it wasn't enough. She had too many unfinished chapters. She'd needed to return to this cottage on the lake, too. Now she had come full circle and could go on. Where would she go from here? Her life had no direction. The future seemed unimportant. It was almost as if this was her destination, which made no sense at all. This was where she would stay—for now—until the Lord gave her direction and moved her on.

She arrived at the little grocery store down the hill from the cottage and limped in for an ice cream cone—a humongous scoop of Rocky Road—and a rest for her hip.

When she finally straggled into the cottage, the pain had reached epic proportions. She should have known better than to overdo it after being so inactive the last three months. She took one of her prescriptions. She wished she didn't need them, but nothing else relieved the severe pain. She had asked the Lord many times to take it away, but He had not done so yet. Accepting that the Lord knew best, she had learned to live with it. She sat down with her journal to organize her thoughts.

Lord, what do You want me to do? What kind of future have You left me? I know You have my best interests in mind, and I'm trying to trust You, but I'm confused and scared. I don't like being so alone. I have no one left in this world. Why couldn't You have taken me home, as well? You have left me with the one thing I wish You had taken—my life. I have no one to cling to but You. Was that Your plan all along, to bring me closer to You? Here I am, Lord, at least what's left of me. What now?

She sat quietly for a few minutes. Then her thoughts shifted, as they often did, and she continued to write.

Oh, Doug, I miss you so much. I knew I depended on you far too much, but I didn't realize to what extent I used you as a crutch.

You would love it here. To see the changing seasons. The leaves are about to turn color. It has been so long that I hardly remember what fall was like. I look forward to the first downy flakes. What? You say I'm a glutton for punishment. I know my hip will hurt in the cold, but if I stay inside I can watch the little diamonds drift to the ground.

She closed her notebook and turned to the window, yawning. Overdoing it on her walk had drained the energy from her. With nothing pressing to do, she gave in and lay on the couch. She sent up a quick prayer that the nightmare wouldn't visit her and dozed off.

૨૦

It was Tuesday when Lori found herself in desperate need of a handyman. The operator hadn't been any help at all. The woman informed her she was not a referral service and didn't know every little dot on the map claiming to be a town.

Everyone who had been at the lake over the weekend was gone now except Garth Kessel. She stared at the number on the gum wrapper. What was the big deal? He had offered to help, and she was definitely in need. He seemed nice enough at the beach fire and wasn't exactly a stranger. Exactly.

So why couldn't she bring herself to dial the number after twenty minutes of holding it? It wasn't as if he were home. He was at work. She had folded it up several times and put it on the counter. She'd even thrown it away once.

"Get a grip, Lori," she finally said aloud. "He'll probably just give you the name of a plumber. Then his civic duty will be done."

She grabbed the phone. His answering machine picked up. Garth's smooth, baritone voice floated through the line. She could picture his deep blue eyes studying her again. The twinkle in them as he told her about the fairy breeze.

Startled by the beep, she quickly hung up. She tried twice more but couldn't bring herself to leave a message and tossed the paper on the counter.

She looked up the Davenports' home number in her address book and left a message on their machine. She would just have to wait to have hot water on the weekend when Mr. Davenport could come up. Her shower this morning had started out lukewarm and become steadily colder.

She received a call around four thirty from Mr. Davenport. He was going to call around and see if he couldn't get someone to come over that evening to look at it. If not, he would be up on Saturday to take care of it.

Twenty minutes later Garth showed up in worn jeans and a white T-shirt. Was he so muscular three nights ago? She supposed he was. She hadn't noticed in the twilight.

"What are you doing here?"

He raised the toolbox in his right hand, causing the muscles in his arm to flex. "The water heater. Mr. Davenport called and said there was a problem with it. Didn't he call to tell you I was coming over?"

Lori shook her head. Whew! It was getting warm all of a sudden. Maybe he should check out the furnace, as well.

"He said he was going to." He stood there looking at her for a few moments. "May I come in?"

"Oh, yeah." Lori stepped aside. Garth filled the room with his very presence.

"This is a nice place." His gaze swept the interior. "I've never been inside before." He looked down at her and raised his eyebrows as if he wanted something. She had no idea what and stared back at him.

"Where's the water heater located?"

Of course! The water heater. "Uh, the bathroom, behind the door." She pointed to the first door on the left.

He gave her a crooked smile that lit his eyes and sent her heart racing. Good thing he turned down the hall before she embarrassed herself. He certainly had better things to do than play fix-it man while she gawked at him.

She felt fidgety standing around waiting for him, so she returned to preparing dinner. She had already coated the chicken and put it in the pan. She was frying all the pieces so she could feast on cold chicken and not have to cook the rest of the week. She had enough if Garth wanted to stay and eat. She shook her head at the ridiculous notion.

As the rice simmered, she pulled fresh vegetables from the fridge: zucchini, mushrooms, onion, and carrots. She washed them and began cutting them.

It would be the nice thing to do to invite him to eat after the work he was doing for her. It was the least she could do. But was it smart? She hardly knew the man. Would Mr. Davenport have sent him over if he didn't trust him? But then Mr. Davenport wasn't a single woman alone in a remote cottage with a man a good eight inches taller than she was, outweighing her by at least seventy-five pounds with muscles popping out of his well-sculptured body.

No. Dinner was definitely out. So why was she still cutting

veggies, enough for an army? She put away the small frying pan and replaced it with the biggest one she could find. After sliding in the cut roughage, she set it aside and placed the refrigerator biscuits on a cookie sheet.

She jumped at the phone ringing and felt silly for it. It was Mr. Davenport.

He explained that he had been held up on the phone and Garth Kessel was on his way over to help. He apologized for not letting her know before Garth arrived. "May I speak with the handyman?"

Handsome man? No. He said handyman. "I'll get him."

Garth's conversation was brief, as well, mostly about the water heater, a couple of comments about the weather, then a "good," "I think so," and "I will" before he hung up. She had the feeling the last comments were referring to her, but she couldn't be sure—just an odd pang in her stomach.

He turned to her. "The water heater needs a part. I'll pick it up tomorrow after school on my way out of town and fix it. I'm sorry you'll be without hot water for another day."

"That's okay. It beats waiting until the weekend." She appreciated his willingness to help her.

He looked at her for a moment, as if debating what he was going to say, reminiscent of the look ten years ago.

She gave him a questioning look in return.

"Why didn't *you* call me?" He pointed to the wrapper on the counter. "You have my number." His voice held a hint of amusement.

The buzzer on the stove sounded. She gladly turned to retrieve the biscuits.

"Saved by the bell." He chuckled.

"Well—I did think about calling you." She turned on the veggies. "But I didn't want to bother you, Mr. Kessel."

"Please call me Garth. Only my students call me mister. And how am I supposed to be neighborly, Lorelei, if I don't know how I can help you? You don't mind if I call you Lorelei, do you?"

She was about to tell him most people called her Lori, but the way *Lorelei* rolled off his tongue like a melody prompted her to say, "Lorelei's fine."

"Please feel free to call if you need anything, anything at all. There aren't many people around here during the week this time of year. If you have any questions about living up here, please ask me." He cocked his head and squinted slightly. "Is there anything else?"

He reminded her of a chivalrous knight who needed a distressed damsel to help. "There is one thing."

In her moment of hesitation he looked at her, silently insisting she ask.

"Do you have a phone book I can borrow? I can't find one around here."

He held out his hands from his sides and smiled. "Just call me the walking, talking yellow pages, at your service," he said with a bow. "What do you want to find?"

"You're the local phone book?"

"I've lived up here year-round for the past five years. To be honest, there isn't much around here to know. The best man for the job won't necessarily be listed in the phone book. If you need a plumber, I know whom to call. If there is a problem with your gas line, I know whom to call. If your roof leaks—"

"You know whom to call. I get the point. It's nothing so grand as any of that. I just need to find a Laundromat."

"That one's easy." He gave her clear, precise directions into Mancelona, even writing them down for future use. "I do have a washer and dryer over at my place if you ever need them and don't want to drive into town."

"Thank you." *But I think I'll use the Laundromat.*

"Anything else?"

"Well. . ."

"Come on, out with it. If I can't answer your question, I'll know who can."

A self-conscious smile tugged at her mouth. "I wanted to

look up churches. I would like to find one to attend while I'm here."

"Churches, hey?"

Ha! She had stumped him.

"There are only three to speak of in Mancelona. St. Peter's run by Reverend Shaw. He's a tall, wiry fellow, a bachelor in his sixties. Pastor Stuart over at First Church is medium height, balding, but his wife and their five children don't seem to mind. And a small group meets in Dotty Fuller's house. She's eighty-seven and always glad to give you her opinion. She's really a sweet lady."

Then he went on to tell her about seven different churches in nearby Kalkaska and the pastors of each, only one of which he claimed not to know much about.

"You're making this up," Lori said.

"I'm wounded." He clutched his chest. "The maiden doth think I lie."

He did seem like a chivalrous knight. "How do you know so much about everyone?"

"I'm a teacher."

"And teachers know everything?"

He shook his head. "Over the past five years I have taught a lot of the area's children. There probably aren't too many families around with at least one child I haven't taught or soon will."

After a moment he said, "So, what will it be?"

"I think I'd like to try that Bible one."

"Great choice." His smile broadened. "Service is at ten; Sunday school starts at eight thirty. I'll pick you up at eight."

She didn't know what to say. "You?"

"I attend Calvary every Sunday and Wednesday nights. You'll like Pastor Rick."

He's a Christian? Realizing she was staring at him, her mouth open, she turned back to her vegetables and started stirring them. *He's a Christian!* The thought delighted her more than she imagined, and before she knew it she said,

"Would you like to stay for dinner? I mean, it's the least I could do after all your help on such short notice."

His smile warmed a bit more. "I would have to be crazy to turn down those heavenly smells and the company of a beautiful lady."

She felt her cheeks warm.

"I'll button up the water heater for now. If it's okay, I'll come by at the same time tomorrow to fix it."

After they sat down and prayed, Lori gazed out at the glimmering water. "I have been curious about something for ten years." She turned back to him and thought she caught a glimpse of something akin to panic in his eyes before he covered it, but she wasn't sure. "Starvation Lake is a strange name. Who would name a lake that? I would think it would turn people away."

Garth spooned vegetables onto his plate. "Most names have historical significance."

"Historical significance?" She passed him the chicken. "Did someone starve here?"

"A whole group of people."

"You're kidding."

"Nope. The first settlers. They mostly ate rabbit all winter."

She looked at him. "If they were eating, how did they starve?" Was this another one of his fairy stories?

"Rabbit, like celery, has negative calories. It takes more to digest it than your body gets out of it."

"Sounds like a good diet food."

He turned toward her. "You do *not* need to diet."

His quick, stern response caught her off guard, and she could feel her cheeks grow warm again.

"I'm sorry. I shouldn't have spoken so harshly. I get tired of seeing these rail-thin girls starving themselves. You look *great* just the way you are."

They talked easily throughout the rest of the meal. She felt comfortable with him. Only one piece of chicken remained, along with a serving of rice and a couple of biscuits. She had eaten more than usual, not because of his comment about dieting but because it was so good. Or was it the company? And how long had it been since he'd had a home-cooked meal?

"Thank you for dinner. It was delicious." He took his plate and glass over to the sink. "But I think I've taken up enough of your time. Besides, I have lesson plans to prepare. I'll see you tomorrow. I'm sorry you'll be without hot water for another day."

"That's okay. I appreciate your fixing it."

"It's not fixed yet, m'lady."

She knew it soon would be and looked forward to seeing him again.

four

Garth sat back in his chair. His last-period students were using the remaining eleven minutes of class to get a head start on the questions he'd assigned. His mind wandered to a particular redhead. He would get to see her again today. She would appreciate his help and probably smile at him.

He drew in a deep breath and could almost smell her soft, flowery perfume, nothing heavy or pungent, rather light and sweet, like the woman who wore it. And green eyes, rich—like an exotic wild orchid he had once seen in a picture. He could wander in their green depths forever. They had left him speechless ten years ago.

He looked forward to hearing her voice also, to hear her say his name. It never sounded so good as it did coming from her lips, soft with a slight lilt.

"Mr. Kessel."

"Call me Garth." He sat up straight, immediately realizing one of his students had addressed him. "Uh—I mean, what?"

"On this part are we supposed to list any three we want?" the short blond girl asked. She reminded him of a pixie.

He read the question three times before he successfully managed to get his brain back in biology class. "List the three main groups."

He glanced up at the clock. Ten minutes! Just like a kid anticipating the end of school.

"Class dismissed."

Looks of bewilderment crossed the faces of his students as they glanced at the clock and back at him.

"Just go quietly."

❧

Lori turned at the knock on the door. Garth arrived as

he'd promised, dressed in much the same way he had been
yesterday, with his toolbox in hand and faded blue jeans; but
instead of a white T-shirt, today's was a soft blue.

"I think these parts will do the trick for that water heater."
He held up a bag then set his toolbox on the floor and the
bag on the counter.

Lori closed the door. "Parts? Is there more than one thing
wrong?"

"It's an old heater. If one part is worn out, others will soon
follow. It's just a precaution. Did you find the Laundromat
all right?" He didn't seem eager to work.

"I haven't gone yet."

"If you have any trouble finding it, let me know. It's easy
to find, so I don't think you'll have a problem. But if there's
anything else you need, don't hesitate to call. There isn't
anything, is there?"

He was a little overeager to help. She wasn't completely
helpless; after all, she'd gone to the school of hard knocks,
graduated near the bottom, but she was learning to take care
of herself. "No, Mr.—I mean, Garth—I'm fine."

"You're sure?" He eyed her.

"The only problem I have is the lack of hot water." *And my
racing heart.*

"That's my cue. I'll get to work on it." He picked up his
toolbox and the bag of parts and headed for the bathroom.

He was finished in less than fifteen minutes. "That should
do it."

"Already? That was quick."

Disappointment welled up in her at his imminent departure.
She had planned to invite him for dinner again to thank
him for his work, but it wouldn't be ready for another thirty
minutes. Would it seem awkward to him to wait so long
after her invitation for dinner to be served? It couldn't hurt
to try.

"Would you like to have dinner? I mean, I have lasagna
in the oven—if you're hungry, that is. It won't be ready for

a while yet, but there's plenty. You've been so nice to give up your time to do this for me. I thought the least I could do is offer you dinner." She was going to start babbling any minute now. *Just be quiet and let the man answer.*

"I love lasagna." He set his toolbox by the door. "In fact, I was wondering how I could finagle my way into staying long enough to make sure the water heater was working properly." He stepped toward the kitchen. "How can I help?"

She tossed the kitchen towel to him. "Wash up, and you can fix the French bread."

Garth washed his hands and took to his assignment with a smile. "Tell me about Lorelei Hayes."

"Pardon?" She put the veggies for the tossed salad in the colander in the sink.

"What you were like in high school? Where you went to college? What you do for a living? How you spend your spare time? Stuff like that."

"There isn't much to tell."

"There has to be something."

Lori took a deep breath and released it. What there was to tell she didn't like. "I missed out on most of high school. I didn't attend college. I do nothing for a living." She hadn't felt like living in a very long time. "And lately I spend a lot of time trying not to feel sorry for myself." She shook her head. "I'm sorry. I feel as if everyone has done so much more living, and I was left behind. I've done nothing. I figure I'm at least seven years behind."

He leaned back on the counter to contemplate her. "How so?"

She wished she had kept her mouth shut, but since she hadn't she might as well go on. "For starters I only got my GED two years ago." She felt a need to explain. "I was in a car accident during my sophomore year of high school. I went through a lot of physical and emotional therapy and more than a dozen operations. It seemed I would recover from one operation, and the doctors were talking about the next one. I wasn't able to go back to school."

"Sounds as if you had a good reason for not finishing, then. It must've been tough."

"Tough's an understatement." She dropped the lettuce she had been cutting up into the bowl one handful at a time. "People always pushing me to do things I didn't want to do, for my own good, of course, but mostly things that caused a tremendous amount of pain." Why did she find it so easy to confide in him?

"What about your friends and family?"

She didn't want to talk about her family or lack of it. "You're slacking off on your duties."

He picked up the butter knife. "I didn't mean to pry."

"That's okay." She mangled another mushroom. "Friends?" she said thoughtfully. "Let's see—there were Chloe and Rachel, Derek, Justine, oh, and what's her name?"

"You can't remember your friend's name?"

"Monica. They weren't my friends. They were my PTs. The closest thing I had to friends."

"PT?"

"Physical therapist. Lyell ended up being my favorite. He did the most for me, or maybe I should say the least."

"It sounds like this Lyell might have worked on your heart as well as your injuries."

"If you're thinking I had a crush on him, no way." She cut through the air with her knife. "I hated him at first, like all the others. He's a retired Marine drill sergeant." She deepened her voice. " 'Quitting is not an option. *Can't* is no longer in your vocabulary.' " She began to clean up the small work area as she spoke. "The really difficult cases were given to him. He said that I was his most challenging patient to date."

"I can't picture you butting heads with a Marine drill sergeant." Garth wrapped the prepared French bread in foil and put it into the oven next to the lasagna.

"I gave him a run for his money. He earned every dollar he made and then some. He wouldn't give up on me even when I had."

The lasagna went as fast as the chicken had the night before. After dinner Garth checked on the hot water and found it steaming. Lori turned down his offer for Wednesday evening church, so he left soon after, probably scared off by all her talk of hospitals and operations. If she had wanted to appall him, she could have become quite graphic and gory. He had seemed genuinely interested, though.

&

Garth surprised Lori by stopping by the following day, but it also pleased her to see him again, if only for a few minutes. She could tell he had come straight from school because he looked very much the teacher in his dress slacks, shirt, and tie. He made a handsome picture standing in her doorway.

"I just stopped by to see if the water heater was working okay for you."

"Works great," she said.

"Oh."

Was that disappointment in his voice?

"It's not too hot?"

"No."

"I could make it hotter if you like."

We certainly don't need any more heat in here. Every time he was around, the cottage suddenly seemed warm. "It's fine just the way it is. Perfect." She wanted to assure him he had done a great job.

"Well, okay. If you have any problems with it, you'll be sure to give me a call," he said, hesitant to leave.

"I promise to call you first thing if I have any problems at all."

"Well, then, I guess I'll see you Sunday." Reluctantly he left.

Reluctantly she let him.

&

On Saturday Lori had a hankering for home-baked cookies, chocolate chip, to be exact. She drove to town to get the ingredients and do a little shopping. She hadn't been in the mood to shop yesterday when she was at the Laundromat. Garth's directions were excellent; even she couldn't get lost. On her way home, though, her left turn came up too quickly, and she had to make a U-turn to get back to it.

Now she smelled the first batch of cookies ready to be taken out. She slid them out of the oven, relishing the aroma. When the last one was on the paper towel to cool, she picked up the first one, broke off a piece, and popped it into her mouth. Mmm. That hit the spot.

I bet Garth would like some of these. She quickly put the remaining eleven cookies on a plate and covered them with plastic wrap, then walked over by way of the beach.

Garth was outside unloading split wood from the back of a pickup truck she hadn't seen before. He had on a pair of denim shorts and a sleeveless T-shirt. The muscles in his back and arms rippled as he took the wood from the truck and stacked it.

It was warmer out here than she thought.

He took a swig of water from his bottle and saw her approaching. He met her at the side of the truck.

"Howdy, neighbor. What brings you over my way?"

"I wanted to thank you for fixing the hot water for me." She held out the cookies.

He smiled. "I thought that's what dinner was for two nights in a row."

"I would hardly call that ample payment. But if you don't want the cookies—" She pulled them back.

"I didn't say that." He plucked the plate from her hands before they were out of reach. He lifted the plastic wrap and took one. "They smell good."

"They taste good, too."

"If you don't mind, I'll judge for myself." His smile told her he had no doubt they were good, and in less than five minutes half of the cookies were gone.

"You're going to spoil your appetite."

"I doubt that." He turned over his wrist to look at his

watch. "But it is almost time for dinner. I need to return Lou's truck. Would you like to come with me to get my SUV? I'll buy you a hamburger in town and an ice cream cone for dessert."

Their gazes locked, and something passed between them. It scared her, but she didn't know why. She had seen him five of the eight days she had been up here, and this was the first awkward moment between them. Was it loneliness or something stronger pulling at her?

"No. I can't." She backed away. "I'm right in the middle of making cookies. I have to go." She turned before he could respond and trotted down the slope across the sand and up the incline to the cottage. She didn't stop until she was safely inside with the door shut behind her.

Why was she running like a scared rabbit being chased by a hunter? He'd only asked her to go for a burger. She had gone over to his place on a whim and realized she shouldn't have gone at all.

❧

Lori wasn't sure if Garth would still pick her up for church after her abrupt departure. But to her delight his dark blue SUV rolled down her steep drive as the clock on the small microwave flipped to eight o'clock. Dressed in a gray suit, he looked dashing. She hoped he wouldn't say anything about yesterday.

"Ready to go?" A smile pulled at his perfect mouth.

She returned his smile. *For over a half hour.* "Ready."

The church was wonderful, just what she was looking for: the people friendly, the music uplifting, and the sermon straight from God's Word. She'd thought she would have to go church hopping for weeks before she found one she liked. But thanks to the *living phone book* who took her, she was able to make a good choice.

She tried to memorize the route home so she could find her way back, but when Garth took an unfamiliar turn she began to question if she knew how to get home at all. This was her first trip into Kalkaska in ten years. "I thought we came from that way." She hadn't meant to speak out loud.

"We did, but I usually grab lunch in town. You don't mind, do you?" He made another turn into a restaurant parking lot.

Once inside, a friendly hostess, Doris, greeted them and immediately chatted familiarly with Garth. Was there anyone he didn't know?

"All she can talk about is Mr. Kessel and her biology class." The hostess guided them to their table.

"I try to make it interesting for the students. If they enjoy it, they'll learn more."

"I don't know how much learning she'll get, but she sure does enjoy your class, along with all her girlfriends." The lady winked at Lori. Lori bit her bottom lip to keep from smiling. She remembered having a crush on her eighth-grade math teacher.

"Girls can do just as well in the sciences as boys," Garth said.

He didn't get it.

Doris laughed. "I don't know about the other sciences, but the girls sure do like *your* biology class." She winked at Lori again and walked away with a huge grin on her face.

Garth furrowed his brows. "What did she mean by that?"

Lori couldn't restrain her smile any longer, and a giggle escaped. "Tell me something, Garth. Do you have a lot of girls in your classes?"

He thought for a moment. "I guess so. But I don't think girls should be discouraged from the maths and sciences just because of their gender. We've had some great female scientists—Madame Curie, Emily Noether, and Ada Lovelace; and Florence Nightingale was more than just a nurse. I'm glad the girls in this area are so interested in science."

"Science?"

"Yes, science." He narrowed his eyes. "What else?"

"Hmm." She raised her menu. "What's good here?"

He put his finger on the top of her menu and lowered it.

"If they don't come to class to learn science, then why are they in my classes?"

Was she the one to enlighten him? She wanted to pull back like yesterday, but at the same time she wanted to move forward.

"If they aren't there for science, what else is there to *your* biology class?" She wanted him to draw the conclusion for himself.

He thought for a moment. "Just me."

At first he appeared clueless. Suddenly, understanding crept into his eyes and spread across his face. "You don't think they're interested in me. I'm at least ten years older than they are, or more."

He was so cute! She wanted to laugh. He thought all those girls were there to learn about science. Chemistry maybe. "You think that will stop a high school crush? Those girls are dreaming about their ruggedly handsome, blond-haired, blue-eyed hunk of a biology teacher."

His expression changed at her complimentary description of him. *Oops!* She could feel the heat spread across her face like a schoolgirl's. She popped the menu back up in front of her.

≈

Garth stared at the back of her menu. He smiled at the thought of her calling him handsome. She hadn't meant to, but she did. He was making progress. After she had run away yesterday, he wasn't sure he hadn't scared her off completely.

He would take whatever small strides he could get. This one would carry him through the week.

≈

Garth arrived at his first class early on Monday morning as usual. He liked to be available to his students if they had any questions. Julie, Amanda, Ami, and Paige were the first to arrive. They sat down giggling and whispering, throwing glances his way. He ignored them and pretended to be busy.

As more students filed into the room, Amanda, a junior and the leader of her little clique, disengaged herself from the group and sauntered up to his desk. She was tall, blond, and pretty enough to be a model. And she knew it, too. She sat on the corner of his desk and stretched her long legs in front of him. Garth rolled his chair back around to the other side of the desk and stood.

"Mr. Kessel, I just don't get chapter 1. I think I may need some special tutoring."

He had never had a student be as overt and forward as Amanda was right now. Then again he'd never had a student like Amanda before, bold and brash.

"I don't think it will take much for me to get it." She sighed and tilted her head.

"Julie seems to understand the material. I recommend you study with her."

"But I was hoping *you'd* help me," she said in a coy baby-doll voice.

"I suggest a study group with Julie." Garth stepped away from his desk. "Class is about to start."

Garth stood behind the demonstration station and looked out at the sea of faces. All the seats were full. Three quarters of his class was made up of females, and half of them were looking up at him with wistful smiles and dreamy eyes. Doris and Lorelei were right. His cheeks warmed.

He couldn't be blushing. Quickly he looked down at the textbook in front of him and absently flipped pages. The bell rang to begin the class, startling him.

How would he ever lecture to this class today? Not on today's topic—cross-pollination!

"Take out a piece of paper—pop quiz."

Moans and groans echoed around the room. By the time the quiz was over, Garth had pulled himself together enough to start his lecture, but the end of class couldn't come too soon.

When the last student left, he dropped his head down on the desk. This was going to be a very, very long day, not to mention the whole week.

five

"Morning," Gretchen said through a yawn.

Garth looked up from the note he was writing as she shook the yawn free. His baby sister padded into the kitchen in her yellow robe and pink fuzzy bunny slippers. The ears flopped back and forth as she shuffled to the cupboard for a mug and poured herself a cup of coffee. She had arrived unexpectedly in the wee hours of the morning.

"I didn't expect you to be up and awake until at least noon."

"Up, yes. Awake, no." She cupped the mug in both hands as though she held a precious stone and sat at the table next to him.

"Sugar?" He scooted the bowl in her direction.

"No, thank you." Another yawn. "I need a straight jolt of caffeine." She sipped the hot brew and grimaced then added four teaspoons of sugar.

Should he tell her the coffee was decaf?

"Wipe that grin off your face. It's too early."

He hadn't realized he was smiling but made an effort to sober his expression.

"That's better." She took another sip then set her mug down. "What are you writing? Killer test questions? I think teachers work far too hard trying to come up with obscure questions to torment their poor students. Go easy on yourself. You don't have to work so hard." She patted him on the shoulder. "Contrary to popular teacher belief, your students won't hate you for being a little lenient on them."

It was obvious whose side she was on, being a college student. "Are you quite through?" he said.

"Mm–hm." She took another gulp.

47

He handed the paper over to her. "It's for you."

"You're giving me a test?" She crinkled up her nose and tried to focus on the words. "This could lose you your favorite-brother status."

As if he, Blake, or Ryan lost any sleep over who was her current favorite. He guessed they were all her favorite. "The hardest question is, are you awake enough to read it?"

"I can read it." She furrowed her eyebrows and pointed to the first word. "There. That says 'Happy.' " She turned her finger on herself. "That's me."

"It seems to be more of a contradiction this morning."

She gave him a forced smile to prove her worth of the pet name. She took another drink of her coffee and turned to the note. "You're going to Kalkaska! I'd love to go. Just let me change my clothes and run a brush through my hair." She jumped up from the table.

Garth caught the chair before it fell over. "Wouldn't you rather go back to bed and sleep some more?"

"With all that caffeine in me? I couldn't sleep now even if I wanted to."

Should he shatter her delusion? Not today. It did his heart good to see his sister perked up. They could talk later about her late-night arrival.

She broke all records and emerged in less than ten minutes dressed in jeans and a white embroidered blouse with her long blond hair drawn up in a high ponytail. Even though she had put on makeup, he could see dark shadows under her eyes.

As expected, she commented when he headed in the opposite direction from Kalkaska.

"The other way's shorter."

"I promised a friend a ride into town."

She leaned her head against the window and yawned. "Oh."

Oh? That was it? She must be tired to utter so little. But she came alive when he turned down the Davenports' drive.

"Ah!" She sat up straighter with a slow grin. "Isn't Lorelei still at the Davenports'?"

Garth rolled his eyes.

"It'll be good to see her again. She seemed nice. How *is* she doing?"

She asked so innocently, but Garth knew she was fishing to see if anything was happening between him and the beautiful redhead. "Fine. I guess." He tried to sound casual, almost disinterested.

"It must be lonely up here for her all by herself."

He put the vehicle in park and turned to her. "Gretchen—" She jumped out before he could tell her not to be pushy. He didn't want Lorelei to be put off.

"I'll go get her."

Garth cut the engine and followed in her wake.

"Look, Bash. Our shirts match." Gretchen stood next to Lorelei. Her blouse was also white with embroidery, but instead of jeans she wore khaki-colored pants. She looked nice. A ray of sunshine on this cloudy day.

"If you two ladies are ready, your coach awaits." Garth made a sweeping gesture toward his truck.

Gretchen abdicated the front seat to Lorelei. Garth held the doors for both ladies, and then they were off. First he stopped to get a muffin and a good strong cup of coffee for his sister, who had yawned in his rearview mirror the whole way.

"I can't believe you fed me decaf coffee and didn't tell me." Gretchen drained her remaining caffeine boost from the cardboard cup.

"You drank the last of the regular coffee when you were here two weeks ago." He pulled beside a parked car, preparing to parallel park.

"And you didn't buy more!"

"I was going to. I wasn't exactly expecting you to sneak in last night unannounced." He put his arm over the back of the seat and maneuvered between the other two cars, resisting the urge to touch Lorelei's shoulder or her hair. Instead he gave Gretchen's cheek a playful squeeze before bringing his arm back to the front. "I think you'll live." He glanced at

Lorelei, who was trying to contain a smile.

Gretchen leaned forward. "Lorelei, don't ever accept a cup of coffee from this guy unless you first find out whether it's leaded or unleaded."

"Okay," Lorelei said carefully.

"Don't tell me you like decaf, too?" Gretchen said.

Lori shrugged her shoulders. "I don't like coffee."

"You're outnumbered, Happy." Garth laughed and climbed out, looking for traffic first.

&

They went to the pharmacy where Lori needed to have her prescriptions filled. The pharmacist was a tall, heavyset man with a strip of dark hair running from one ear around the back of his head to the other, and the top shined as much as the highly polished floor under her feet. After a few minutes of friendly catch-up chatter, Garth introduced her.

She was grateful when Garth and Gretchen gave her some privacy by wandering through the store. She didn't like to make a big issue out of her aches and pains and would like nothing better than to forget about them if she could.

The pharmacist pulled a pair of reading glasses out of his shirt pocket and settled them on the end of his nose. He studied each of the prescription bottles. "Where are these from?" He peered at her over the top of his glasses. Just like a bug under a microscope.

"Florida."

His eyebrows shot up. "You're a long way from home."

"It's not home anymore." Her throat tightened with the familiar feeling of melancholy.

"I'll have to call the prescribing physician on these. Since it's Saturday he may be difficult to reach."

Lori pulled a letter from her purse. "Dr. Torren gave me this letter before I left Florida. He said it would make it easier to get my prescriptions filled. I don't need them yet. I can pick them up later in the week." She wished she didn't need them at all, but she did and only took them when absolutely necessary.

"This letter will help," he said after studying it for a minute. "Let's say Wednesday to be safe."

Lori searched the drugstore for her two companions and found them by the greeting cards. Gretchen appeared to be reading one out loud to Garth. His smile broadened, but he looked confused. Gretchen was practically doubled over from laughing so hard. Tears streamed down her cheeks.

"What's so funny?" Lori asked Garth, because Gretchen was in no condition to talk.

Garth shrugged his shoulders. "I have no idea. I think the caffeine has gone to her head."

Gretchen held out the card to Lori. She took it from her because she couldn't focus on the jiggling object. On the front was a pathetic-looking man with a bouquet of roses behind his back ringing a doorbell. Inside it read, "I'm sorry."

Lori looked up at Garth. She didn't get the joke.

Garth shook his head and put the card back on the rack.

"Oh, I want to buy it." Gretchen plucked the card from its slot. "Don't mind me. It's just my warped sense of humor."

"That's not all that's warped," Garth said as his sister headed for the cash register.

"I heard that," she called back over her shoulder.

It would be an entertaining day spending time with this brother-sister team.

Once back out at Garth's vehicle, Gretchen rubbed her hands together. "Where to next?"

"I'm finished in town." Garth turned to Lori. "Is there any-place else you need to go?"

"No." She looked at him, curious. Other than buying coffee for Gretchen, he hadn't done anything in town.

Garth held her with his intense blue gaze. "Who's up for lunch? My treat."

"Can we eat at the Dunes? I haven't been there in ages," Gretchen said.

"Sounds great. Is that all right with you?" Garth waited for her reply.

Her stomach did a little happy, skippy thing. "I guess. What are the Dunes?"

"You've never been to the Sleeping Bear Sand Dunes?" Gretchen leaned forward over the seat. "Oh, Bash, we have to take her."

She had called him Bash earlier. What was behind the nickname?

Less than an hour later, when they arrived at the Dunes, Lori was in awe at the mountain of sand stretched out before her. It was indeed a huge sand dune. "How did all this sand get here?"

"God," Gretchen said simply and headed for the snack bar and another cup of coffee.

Before Lori knew it, the three of them were trudging up the sandy slope. The dune seemed to stretch on forever, and her weary legs ached with each labored step; but the destination was well worth the pain. It was magnificent, all this sand, dwarfed by the gleaming waters of majestic Lake Michigan. A touch of the Almighty. She made some mental notes of the inspiring sites she would write down later.

After an hour of wandering around, Gretchen challenged them to a race down the hill.

"I don't think that's a good idea," Garth said, glancing at Lori.

Did he suspect something about her hip?

"Are you afraid a couple of girls can beat you?" Gretchen said.

"No. I—"

"Then prepare to be beaten, bro." She crouched to a starting position as did Lori.

Lori hadn't raced since before the acci—in a very long time. This would be fun, and she would ignore her hip if it acted up.

"On your mark—get set—go," Gretchen said in a single breath. She and Lori sprang forward before Garth was ready.

"You asked for it," came Garth's deep voice behind them.

It didn't take long before Garth passed them and was halfway down the hill. Gretchen also rapidly outdistanced her, but that didn't put a damper on her fun. At the bottom they found a bench to empty their shoes of sand while they caught their breath.

Later, when Gretchen suggested pizza and a video, Lori leaped at the idea. She was having too much fun for this day to end.

When Garth went in for the pizza, Lori opted to stay in his vehicle, as did Gretchen. Gretchen leaned forward, resting her arms on the back of the seat. "So are you staying at the lake long?"

She hadn't a clue what she was doing. Healing for now, but what direction for the future? "For a few weeks."

"Great. You'll have to go to Mackinac Island since you'll be here for a while"

"What's on Mackinac Island?"

"It's a really cool place. No cars are allowed; everything's horse and buggy or bicycles. There are a lot of cute little shops and tons of fudge. Have you seen the movie *Somewhere in Time*? It was filmed on the island."

She shook her head. A place with no cars? That sounded like her kind of place. "It sounds quaint. Where is it?"

"It's a couple of hours north from here between the upper and lower peninsulas."

Lori didn't know enough about Michigan to know where the two peninsulas were. "How do I get there?"

Gretchen shook her head. "I'm the last person on earth you want to ask for directions—unless you're trying to get lost—then I'm your girl. Are you doing anything next Saturday?"

Lori gave herself a mental shake at the rapid change in subjects. "I have nothing planned." She wanted to find out where this island sanctuary without cars was. "What did you say the island is called?" Maybe she could find it on a map. Garth opened the driver's door with a flat pizza box in one hand.

"Bash, is Mom's copy of *Somewhere in Time* still at the cottage?"

Lori reached over and took the piping-hot pizza from him so he could climb in easier.

"Yes. You know she only watches it up here."

"Lori has never seen it or been to Mackinac Island."

Garth looked at Lori. She shrugged her shoulders in response. She hadn't lived in Michigan long enough to see the sights.

"Don't they close the island at the end of September?" Gretchen asked her brother.

He pulled out into traffic, what little there was. "I'm not sure. Either that or October."

"To be safe let's say September. Next Saturday you can take her there."

Garth opened his mouth to say something, but Gretchen went on. "She's not busy. I already asked her."

So that's why Gretchen was asking about next weekend. She was setting up a date between her and Garth. Her face warmed, and she looked away.

"I know you didn't make it up there this summer, so you haven't had your fudge fix."

"Gretchen, I don't—"

"You don't have plans next Saturday, do you?"

"No, but—"

"Great. Then you can pick her up early, let's say six thirty; catch the first ferry, spend the day there, and get the last ferry back."

Garth rolled his eyes in resignation.

"You did say you wanted to go, didn't you?" Gretchen spoke to Lori this time.

"Well. . .yes," she said hesitantly. Mackinac Island sounded enchanting. No cars, horse-drawn carriages, quaint streets lined with dozens of little shops. It sounded like the next best thing to heaven. She did look forward to visiting it but felt awkward being pushed into it this way.

"Then it's settled. Garth will pick you up at six thirty next Saturday morning." Gretchen folded her hands in her lap and sat back, pleased with herself.

Lori glanced at Garth. He nodded his approval. "The leaves will be starting to turn. The island should be beautiful. And they do have the best fudge." He smiled and wiggled his eyebrows.

❧

Garth's cottage was considerably larger than the Davenports', and she noticed a stair railing leading down. With a piece of pizza in her hand Gretchen took Lori on a tour of the place.

The kitchen was large and open and shared space with the dining area that was occupied by a huge oak table pushed up against the wall. Next to the dining room was the living room with two couches, a rocking chair, a fireplace on the far wall, and the extra dining room chairs scattered around the room.

Gretchen pointed out three bedrooms on that floor then three more on the lower level. The rec room had a couch and a Ping-Pong table, and in the far corner stood a weight machine. So that was how Garth kept in such good shape.

After the quick tour they sat down and polished off the rest of the pizza before the movie began. Gretchen opened a bag of chips and one of pretzels and rummaged through the refrigerator until she located some dip. They sat on the couch opposite the TV with Gretchen in the middle, though she had tried to sit on the end.

The movie was a tragic love story. Love searched for and found, love lost, and love that had waited a lifetime to return. And it was all set on Mackinac Island. She wanted to see it for herself now more than ever. By the end Lori and Gretchen had tears coursing down their cheeks.

Garth handed them a box of tissues. "Did you two enjoy the movie?"

Lori felt embarrassed to become so emotional over a movie and quickly dried her eyes.

Gretchen playfully backhanded her brother in the chest.

"Don't act like that."

"Like what?" He put his hands up to feign surrender.

"Like you are completely unaffected by this movie. I've seen you cry at the end before."

"Me?" His single word dripped with innocence.

Gretchen growled. "Yes, you." She pulled the pillow out from behind her and bopped him with it. "You are the most sensitive guy I know!" She started to swat him with the pillow again.

Garth held up his arms. "Uncle! I give! I do like the movie."

"And?"

"And what?" He smiled.

"And you have cried at it before." She poised the pillow over her head.

He raised his eyebrows in teasing disbelief, and she smooshed the pillow into his face.

"Okay, okay!" he said, laughing.

Seeing the two interact in fun tugged at Lori's heartstrings. She missed Doug and felt the overwhelming urge to start crying again. It was only because of her heightened emotions from the wonderfully sappy movie, she told herself. She had to go—*now*.

"Thank you both for a wonderful day and the movie—and the sand dunes." She grabbed her purse and headed for the door. She could tell they were both taken aback by her abruptness. "I have to go." She hurried out the door before either one could stop her.

six

Garth stared at the closed door for several seconds, wondering what had happened. He turned to Gretchen.

She shrugged and answered his unspoken question. "I have no idea. I suppose one of us should go after her."

"I'll go. You don't have your shoes on." Not that if she had shoes on, it would have stopped him.

He pushed off the couch and exited, jogging to catch up to Lorelei's hurried pace. "Lorelei, wait—please."

She stopped and turned slightly toward him as he came up beside her but kept her gaze averted.

"Is everything all right? You left kind of suddenly." He half expected her to run away. She was so flighty around him. Since he could think of nothing he had done, he figured it was her way, and he'd take things slow.

"I just had to go." Her voice sounded a little strained. "I didn't realize how late it was."

A quarter to nine? "If Gretchen or I did something to offend you, we're sorry."

She looked up at him, startled. "No. You and Gretchen have been more than kind."

He could see tears brimming in her eyes but didn't want to embarrass her by mentioning them. He knotted his hands into fists to keep from wrapping his arms around her until her tears were gone. Was it the movie that put those tears there or something else? "If you ever need to talk—"

"No, no." She looked at his chin, the lake, the sand, anywhere except at his eyes. "I just needed to go."

He nodded and let her go, watching until she disappeared up the path beside the cottage. A small amount of satisfaction washed over him when a light came on inside. Though he still wanted to make sure she was safe, he had to believe she was and would be fine. With a prayer for her he turned and headed back home.

When he entered the cottage he turned his attention from one upset woman to another. Gretchen sat on the edge of the couch with the card she had bought in her hand, but this time she wasn't laughing. He sat down beside her. "Not quite as funny as it was earlier."

She burst into tears and leaned against his shoulder. As quickly as her tears began they stopped, and she pulled away from him, balling up her fists. "I'm so mad at him." She swiped at her tears. "It served him right to be left standing there with a bunch of dumb flowers. I'm glad I know, though. It's as if I've been set free, but it still hurts."

His sister was a torrent of emotions. This was going to be a long night. "You want to back up and fill in a few of the blanks so I can follow along? I assume 'him' is Lonny?"

"Of course Lonny. Who else?"

"As I recall, you two broke up two weeks ago; that's why you were here then."

"We did, or rather I broke up with him." Her voice got soft and dreamy. "But the past two weeks he's been so sweet." She lingered on the last word.

Uh-oh. That sounded like trouble, as if he were trying to make up for a transgression.

"Until—" She jumped up from the couch and frowned. "I can't believe I was actually considering that jerk's proposal."

"W—wait a minute. P—proposal?"

"Insincere proposal, no doubt," she spat out.

"So you told him no?"

"I said I needed time to think."

"When were you planning to give him your answer?"

After a moment's hesitation she said in a small voice, "Last night."

"But something went wrong, and you ended up here."

"Lon is such a—such a—a. . ."

He could tell she was searching for the worst possible thing to call him; he wondered what she would find.

"Man!" She stomped her stockinged foot.

Well, now, that was terrible. He was a man.

She started pacing. "He is the lowest of the low. He could play handball against the curb. No, that would be too big. He could fit under a pregnant earthworm."

Garth had to say her name three times before his voice penetrated her tirade. "Hold on a minute." Everything so far was emotional. "Let's go back. You never did tell me why you broke up with him in the first place."

She rolled her head upward. "His wandering eyes." Her tone was dramatic. "Even when we were out together, he would look at other girls or tell me about the pretty girl who sat next to him in one of his classes. Of course she wasn't as pretty as I was, he always told me." She gestured widely with her hands as she spoke. "I told him I didn't like it. Then he would say"—her tone dropped to mimic a man's—" 'God made pretty women for guys to look at. It's only natural. It's not like I'm asking any of them out. It's like window-shopping.' "

Garth narrowed his eyes. *Shopping for what?*

She pressed her hands to her temples. "I couldn't take it any longer."

"Why did you put up with it at all?"

"Because I was in love with him. And he loved me."

"I doubt that."

"I do, too. At least now I do. But I believed it up until yesterday. It wasn't so much that he *scanned the scenery* but that he didn't seem to care how it made me feel. The final straw was last night. He was supposed to pick me up, and we were going to go out to dinner and talk. I ran down the hall to borrow a hair band from a friend who lives in my dorm. When I came out, Lon was at my door ready to knock, but he was looking the other way at a girl walking away from him. Probably leering. She turned the corner, and then he knocked on my door." She picked up the card that had fallen to the floor and shook it. "Just like this, with a stupid four-dollar bouquet behind his back, as if that would fix everything." She ripped the card up and started to cry again.

Garth stood and put his arms around her.

"I left him there. He never knew I saw. I hid in my friend's room until he was gone." She pushed away from him. "Which, by the way, only took him seventeen minutes. He begged me to marry him, and he waited only seventeen minutes. My first impulse was to go home, but I couldn't face Mom and Dad. They never did like Lon."

"I never heard them say one negative thing about him. Although it appears they rightfully could have."

"And they never would. It was more what they didn't say and how they acted. I knew they didn't approve of him."

"So you came up here to sort things out."

"I did that on the way." She gave a dismissive wave of her hand. "Mostly I thought about what I said to Lori about you the night of the get-together at Shawn's."

"What!"

"Oh, don't look so scared. You remember I told her how great you were. I got to thinking about what makes you so different, so much better than someone like Lon. You are kind and compassionate, loyal and honorable, and you consider other people's feelings."

"I think you're prejudiced because I'm your *favorite* brother." He grinned.

"Garth, why did you come back so quickly? Why didn't you go over to her place and find out what was wrong?" Her look was intense and inquisitive.

"She didn't want to talk, and I didn't want to embarrass her by pushing. I prayed for her, though." *I hope she's feeling better and able to sleep.*

"I rest my case." She had a forlorn, far-off look. "I wonder if I'll ever find a man as thoughtful and considerate as you."

At twenty she was worried about finding a life partner.

"Don't use me as a comparison. I'm only human. You should be seeking Jesus."

"Yes, I know." She turned to him. "But unless a guy is as kind and thoughtful as you, he's out." She gestured with her thumb like an umpire.

They talked until after two in the morning.

"Thanks, Garth, for talking with me. You always did understand me best." She yawned into the back of her hand.

Understand? He couldn't claim he understood her at all. Even though he had four sisters and a mother, women were still a mystery. This one in particular. He gave up a long time ago trying to understand his baby sister and just accepted her as is—with giggles and tears alike.

He strolled outside to the tree and prayed again for the woman he wanted the chance to understand.

❧

The butterflies in Lori's stomach fluttered more furiously the closer it got to eight o'clock. She had debated whether or not to call Garth and say she wasn't going to church this morning or she would drive herself. But that would only emphasize her abrupt departure last night and make her more uncomfortable.

She knew all she needed last night was a good cry, and cry she did until she fell asleep. But she was comforted in the fact she was not alone. Jesus was with her, feeling her pain and loss, suffering with her and for her. She had slept well and felt refreshed.

She closed her eyes to lift up her praise for the day. *Thank You, Jesus, for always being with me. No matter what the circumstances I'm not alone.*

At eight o'clock on the dot Garth's truck rolled down the drive with Gretchen in the passenger seat. Lori felt a little awkward during the ride to church, but having lunch together after the service helped her relax. Then she hugged Gretchen and wished her well on her return to school after the weekend.

When it came time for the Wednesday night meeting at church, she had almost forgotten she had fled Garth's house a few days earlier. And she was looking forward to visiting Mackinac Island on Saturday.

On Thursday Josie called to tell her she and her parents were coming up for the weekend to prepare the cottage for winter. They needed to bring in the dock, replace the screens with storm windows, and stack firewood. She would have to cancel her plans to go to Mackinac Island with Garth.

She knew she should call him as soon as she hung up with Josie. But she feared her disappointment would steal into her voice. Or, worse, she might hear no disappointment in his. He may be glad to be off the hook. So she waited until the next day and called while he was at work to recite her rehearsed message.

&

Garth had an uneasy feeling on Friday when he came home from work and found his old Pontiac once again parked by the cottage. Gretchen was back, and that wasn't all. She had all her belongings stacked to the roof.

"You quit school!"

"Don't be mad at me, Bash," she said sweetly with a puppy-dog look. "I thought you of all people would understand."

"Understand? No, I don't understand. You are a complete anomaly. What did Dad and Mom have to say about this?"

She bit her bottom lip and averted her eyes to her shoes and not because of the sequins and stars scattered over them.

Garth let out a groan. "They don't know, do they?"

"Not exactly," she said quietly.

His nerves tensed immediately. "Translated, no! And you came up here to hide." He raked his hands through his blond hair. "Why, Happy? Is this about Lonny?"

"No. He's almost quit being a pest."

"Then why quit school?"

She sighed. "There I sat in Ed 301 while Professor Black droned on, wondering why I was there. Ever since I can remember, I was told I would be a teacher. I played school with my dolls and stuffed animals, so naturally that meant I was destined to be a teacher. I accepted it. It was easy." She looked intently at him. "Do you know a lot of people play school who aren't even education majors?"

She walked over to the window, holding herself around the waist, and looked out. Her voice became distant. "I don't want to be a teacher."

She paused then turned quickly to him. "I have nothing against teachers. I have a family full of them. It seems we Kessels either have to be one or marry one. You're a teacher, Dad's a professor, and Mom teaches third grade." She ticked each person off on her fingers as she listed them. "Robin is a special education teacher, Mike's a principal, Pete's an administrator, and Audrey is so close to finishing her degree. But even if she never becomes a teacher, that's okay because she married one. And Ryan will be a student forever—that's almost as good! Oh, and let's not forget Ruth. She homeschools her and Blake's two girls."

She was really worked up now.

"You didn't have to quit school," Garth said more calmly than he felt. "You could have simply changed majors."

"How unthinkable," she said, her face red and her fists balled, "if a Kessel should not have a college degree!"

"An education is important," Garth said.

"Lori doesn't have a degree. She barely has a high school diploma."

He glared at her, frowning. "She has had a difficult life. And we weren't talking about her."

"It's not that I don't want to get a degree—in whatever. It's just not for me right now. I want to do other things. I want to break the Kessel mold, be an original."

"You've already succeeded." He clenched his mouth. "What things can't wait another two years until you finish?"

"Life. I want to go places. . .see things. . .have adventures. I was thinking about maybe being a missionary or joining the peace corps." The excitement showed in her eyes as well as her voice.

"The peace corps?" he said. "You can't exactly take your curling iron into the jungle." He could not picture his baby sister living in rugged conditions.

"Actually I'm most interested in working on a cruise ship—as a cruise director or something. I could see new places and meet new people."

Only Gretchen could lump a luxury cruise ship with the peace corps and missionary work. She was an anomaly. He agreed to let her stay—but only if she called their parents.

৵

Lori stewed all day about the message she'd left on Garth's machine. Now she wished she hadn't been so chicken and had talked to him in person.

Garth couldn't have been home more than a few minutes when Lori's phone rang. Garth offered to help Mr. Davenport, and she promised to pass along the offer to him.

Lori tucked her hair behind her free ear. "I'm sorry to have to cancel on Mackinac Island."

"That's okay. It's open through October. I checked. The trees should have more color this coming weekend—that is, if you don't have other plans."

She could hear the tentativeness in his words. Her heart wanted to shout, "Yes, I want to go with you," but her head said, "Don't be foolish." She knew she should discourage any kind of relationship from budding, but she really wanted to go. "No, I don't have any other plans. Mackinac Island would be wonderful." She managed to sound casual and not too excited.

"I've never been to the island this late in the season. I look forward to it."

She did, too, and tried to tell herself it was only the trip she was eager for and not the company.

৵

Garth came home on Monday to find his answering machine

blinking with seven messages. He didn't receive seven messages in a week, let alone in one day; and besides, Gretchen was around. Or was she? Her car was still here, but she was suspiciously absent.

He pressed the PLAY button and sifted through his mail but stopped at once when he heard his mother's worried voice. Five of the messages were from her, one from his father, and one from another sister—all inquiring about Gretchen's whereabouts.

He looked at his watch. His mother's last call had come only five minutes earlier. He left the cottage to search for his wayward sister before his mother called again. Since she hadn't driven her car she would be close by, and she drew strength from people. Who was around she could go to and hide behind so he wouldn't make a fuss? Lorelei. To his surprise he was already halfway to her place. On the beach he walked around dock sections stacked on the larger dock that floated on the lake in the summer. He had helped Mr. Davenport bring them in over the weekend.

He walked up the wooden logs set into the ground as steps along the side of the cottage and knocked on the door. His ire melted away when Lorelei answered the door with a smile.

"Would you like to come in?"

"Yes, I would, but I can't. I'm looking for Gretchen. Have you heard from her?"

"You've come to the right place." She motioned him in.

Gretchen was surprised to see him but put on a sweet smile and said innocently, "Bash. We were just about to head into town and get a burger and maybe catch a movie."

And you were hoping to escape before I got here. For a moment he thought about taking up the offer and not making a fuss. He wouldn't mind spending time with Lorelei. Instead he looked back at Gretchen just as innocently. "Can't. We have a family emergency."

"It can wait until later. I'm hungry."

"No, it can't. Mom's sick."

"What?" She stood.

Garth apologized to Lorelei for both of them, and they left.

"Mom's sick? What's wrong?" Gretchen asked as they headed down toward the beach.

"She's sick with worry over her missing youngest daughter." His tone was curt.

"Garth!" She swatted at his arm. "You had me worried. I thought something was wrong."

"There is something wrong. Mom is worried sick about you, and you don't seem to care."

She dropped her head and said softly, "It's not that I don't care. I'm just not ready to talk to them yet. I don't know what to say."

"Tell them the truth."

"Garth, would you call and tell them I'm here and I'll call next week?"

"No. This is your mess; you have to own up to it. Right now Mom will be happy just to know you are all right. You were supposed to call on Saturday before coming over to the Davenports'."

"I did."

He gave her a sideways glance. She obviously hadn't told them anything significant.

The phone was ringing when they entered. "That's probably for you," Garth said, but Gretchen moved away from the ringing phone. He stared after her as the machine picked up, and soon his mother's distressed voice cut through the air.

He grabbed the phone and heard his mother let out a big sigh when he answered. She was glad she was finally speaking to a person. She poured out her concerns and how she was unable to reach Gretchen. "Her roommate says all her things are gone, and she hasn't seen her since Thursday. You don't think she moved in with that boyfriend of hers? She can be so unpredictable."

"Yes, Mom, she can be very unpredictable." He glared at his baby sister. "But, no, I don't think she would move in with Lonny. She wouldn't do that." *I hope.*

Gretchen's mouth dropped open in shock. He was glad to see the thought bothered her. He crooked his finger at her to come over to the phone. She shook her head.

"I didn't think so, but you know how she can be, so flighty and erratic. The most worrisome to me of all you children. I didn't feel old until she grew up. Where could she be? You haven't heard from her, have you?"

"As a matter of fact, Mom, I have."

"Oh, thank the Lord! Where is she? Is she there? Is she all right?"

"She's fine, Mom. She's right here."

"May I talk to her?"

The relief in his mother's voice tore at him. "Of course you can." He held out the phone to his reluctant sister. She stared at it but didn't move. He set it down on the counter and walked out. She would have to deal with it now. But where would he go?

His first inclination was Lorelei's. What excuse could he give for returning? Gretchen had promised to go to dinner with her. Maybe she would settle for him? But if his offer sounded too much like a date, she would likely turn him down as she had before. If he made it sound casual, as if she would be doing him a favor, she might concede. By the time he reached her door he'd figured out how to ask—or rather suggest.

"Is your mom okay?" she asked.

"She'll be fine now that she can talk to Gretchen." He shifted uncomfortably. "Would you like me to have dinner with you?"

Her eyebrows shot up.

"I mean, I'll take you to dinner. . . ." Why was it so difficult to think straight around her?

"What about Gretchen?"

"She can't make it. She'll be on the phone for a while. I'll bring her back something, and I know you haven't eaten." That wasn't how he'd wanted to say it, so now she would politely turn him down.

"Gretchen and I had a hankering for a thick, juicy burger with greasy fries and a fat-filled milkshake," she said lightly with a smile. "Are you sure you can handle that?"

"I live for cholesterol."

"You are not exactly dressed for a burger joint."

Was she trying to dissuade him from going? If she were willing to go out with him for whatever reason, he wouldn't pass it up. "I can change. I'll be back in a few minutes." He turned to leave.

"Oh, and I was planning to drive," she said, her eyes sparkling, "my car."

"Oh." He looked at her then cleared his throat. "I'll be right back." She was trying to get rid of him, but even being seen in her purple car couldn't discourage him from being with her.

When he arrived at his place, Gretchen was still on the phone, making plans to head down to their parents' house the next day. After changing, he motioned to her he was going out. She nodded and waved him on.

"I'll bring you back something," he whispered.

"Thank you," she mouthed.

He sensed she was thanking him for more than food. He closed the door behind him and headed back to Lorelei's.

ଈ

Lori mentally patted herself on the back for her self-control. She had kept a straight face as she told Garth they would be using her car, her *very purple* car. His shocked look was precious. He didn't want to hurt her feelings by insulting her car, but she looked forward to seeing this handsome, rugged man cowering in it. Though purple was a vogue color, not everyone liked it. He was so much like Doug.

She burst out laughing when she saw his SUV come down

her drive. He was trying to get out of riding in her car, but she wouldn't let him off the hook so easily. She curbed her laughter and put on what she hoped was a casual look.

When they walked out to his truck, she feigned surprise. "Aren't we taking my car?"

"I thought I'd drive since I know my way around better."

That was smooth. "Don't you trust my driving?"

"I'm sure you're a fine driver. It's just that. . ." His words trailed off as she looked up at him innocently. He took her hand and placed his keys in it. "Here—you can drive."

It proved he trusted her to drive, but it wasn't the reason he didn't want to take her car. "If I'm going to drive, I'd be more comfortable driving my car."

He started to speak several times but didn't. He couldn't admit it.

"I understand." She smiled. "Really, I do. It's a macho guy thing, right? No self-respecting guy would be caught dead in a car that looks like an overgrown grape."

"Something like that." He let out a sigh of relief. "I'm sorry."

"It's okay. You only had to say you didn't want to ride in a ridiculous purple car. Besides, I'm a terrible driver. I was going to let Gretchen drive." She tossed his keys in the air and walked around the truck. She heard him catch them, and suddenly he was by her side, opening her door.

"You were going to ask me to drive all along, weren't you?"

She answered with a smile. Garth was as careful a driver as Doug had been, and she felt comfortable with him behind the wheel.

What she'd wanted to know was how badly he wanted to go with her. She was pleasantly surprised he hadn't called to back out completely. She had given him plenty of opportunities. Why did she care anyway if he wanted to go with her? It shouldn't matter, but it did. Nothing could come of a relationship between them; she would make sure of that and keep him at arm's length.

seven

Lori looked into Garth's critical face. She had awakened early, anxious for today, and taken extra care with her clothes and her appearance. She had debated over what to wear and changed three times. She finally decided on her long denim skirt, a short-sleeved white blouse, and a tapestry vest with a pair of comfortable flats. Nice but not overdone. She had even found many things for which to praise God.

But now her emotions belly flopped onto the floor at Garth's disapproving look. Why did she care what he thought? It wasn't as if they were anything more than friends.

"You're going to want to dress warmer." He eyed her up and down. "Not that you don't look great, but the island can be chilly this time of year. Jeans and a sweater would be better."

He leaned on the front doorframe while she retreated into her bedroom to change. She shed her well-chosen clothes and slipped on a pair of jeans and a thin, white cotton sweater with her vest over it, then wriggled her feet into a pair of white canvas sneakers.

She stood before him for his approval but found him less than impressed. "You have nothing warmer, a heavier coat, perhaps?"

"No." She was surprised at the hurt from his rejection. "It doesn't get that cold in Florida."

"This is Michigan, the cold North, not tropical Florida."

"You're wearing a short-sleeved shirt." He had on jeans and a blue-and-green-striped golf shirt that complemented his eyes, along with tennis shoes.

"I have a sweatshirt and coat in my truck."

"If you think it's going to be that cold, maybe I shouldn't

70

go." She was beginning to doubt the wisdom of going at all. This was stepping over the line. No, her heart was dragging her over the line to someplace she knew she shouldn't go.

"Come on. I have an idea. You'll be fine." He ushered her out before she could retreat.

They drove over to his place, and she waited while he ran inside. He climbed back in and placed two sweaters and a sweatshirt on her lap.

"Pick whichever one you want." He headed back up the drive.

"Thank you." She decided on the heather gray sweatshirt with the college insignia on it. As she put the sweaters in the back, she noticed a lopsided grin pull at Garth's mouth at her choice.

People would think she had gone to college. They would never guess only two years ago she had gotten her GED. There had been no time for an education, not that she really cared. It was Doug who had forced her to get her GED and learn to drive. That was when she started to heal mentally, getting back some of what the accident had robbed from her. She could never get it all back, but she had stopped being the victim, most of the time.

His deep voice pulled her back to the present.

"I'm sorry. What?"

"I was wondering what you do that allows you so much time off to stay up here?"

She found it hard to comprehend when he smiled at her that way. "Do?"

"Yes, your job." His gaze darted in her direction.

"Job?"

"I thought maybe you did some sort of freelance work." He glanced at her again. "You sit out at the picnic table writing."

"You've seen me?"

"Journalist, perhaps?" He looked at her again.

She wished he would stop doing that and keep his eyes on the road. "No, not me."

"A poet."

Seen me? He watched her? The thought of someone watching her should bother her, but it didn't. "Unfortunately I don't have to work."

"Unfortunately? Independently wealthy doesn't sound too bad."

It did to her. "I was awarded a large settlement for my 'pain and suffering.' The boy who plowed into us was drunk or high on something and from a very wealthy family. The money could never replace having my life destroyed and my future ripped away." She turned away from him. Why had she blurted all that out?

He touched her shoulder. "I'm sorry."

"Thanks. It's all right." She pushed the old hurts back. She wouldn't allow them to spoil today. She lived far too much in the past but couldn't help herself. The Lord had been good to bring her back to Michigan, and she would focus on that.

When they reached Mackinaw City, Garth parked in one of the ferry lots. "Don't forget this." He handed her the sweatshirt she had laid on the seat beside her.

She stepped out of the truck, and goose bumps immediately rose on her arms from the chilly breeze. She slipped the sweatshirt over her head. Garth, too, had put on his sweatshirt but stuffed his coat in his knapsack. His sweatshirt was identical to hers. She debated whether or not to use one of the sweaters instead, but it was too late. He had locked the truck. She pretended not to notice but was sure he knew they matched.

She and Garth sat on the first level with a handful of other passengers for the sixteen-minute hydroplane ferry ride over to Mackinac Island. The island was breathtaking, all decked out in an array of autumn colors with the white Grand Hotel stretched against the golds, oranges, and reds.

Lori stepped off the ferry and into another century. Up ahead, where the dock met land, stood a coach with a matching pair of chestnut brown horses. On its maroon, hard-shell side were the words *The Grand Hotel*. Beside that coach was another quite different carriage, red and yellow with plastic sides rolled up to the soft roof. *Taxi*. A pair of dapple gray horses stood hitched to it. The drivers of both sat patiently in their seats and smiled at her as she and Garth passed them.

Garth guided her up the short incline to the main street. "There's a bike shop over here."

She looked up one end of the street and then the other. Quaint shops lined both sides, each one unique—some wood, some brick, each a different height and style. "I want to go in every shop."

"Then we should forgo biking around the island, taking the carriage tour, or visiting the fort, the Grand Hotel, and the Butterfly House."

She turned to him quickly. "I want to do all those, too."

He chuckled. "You can't. My mom and sisters determined on one trip to go in every single shop and couldn't do it. They got through about half and felt rushed. There are shops on the side streets and the streets above."

She sighed in defeat.

"I suggest we do the sightseeing things this morning— biking around the island and taking the carriage tour. Those will give you the broadest perspective of the island. And then one other—"

"The butterflies."

He nodded. "The butterflies it is. Then after lunch, if you'll trust me to pick out a few good shops my mom and sisters like, we'll hit as many as possible."

Her eyes rounded. "There's so much to see and do here."

His mouth pulled up on one side. "I'll just have to bring you back more than once."

Her insides fluttered at his earnestness.

Garth guided her to a nearby bike shop where he rented a tandem bicycle to pedal the eight miles around the island.

"You drive." He motioned for her to get on the front of the two-seat bike.

She hesitated. "I don't know where to go."

"See this street? Go that way"—he pointed in one direction down the road then back the other direction—"until you come around there."

That seemed pretty easy, a circle.

"And if you're nice, I'll do all the pedaling up the hill."

"And what if I get us lost?"

"I think that's physically impossible. Even Gretchen couldn't get lost."

The road ran along the beach a few yards from the water. After several minutes they paused to gaze out at the glistening blue green water. A short way up the road Garth stopped so they could look at Arch Rock, more than a hundred feet above the water. She could see right through to the sky that had become stormy. Wind and water had eroded the soft rock below, leaving the hard breccia rock to form an arch. She guessed it was even more enchanting with the golds and reds of the foliage and the occasional leaf drifting down.

"Legend says a beautiful Indian maiden called Ne-Daw-Mist met a handsome brave of the sky spirits," Garth said in an ethereal tone. "They fell in love but were forbidden to marry by her cruel father. He beat her and tied her to a high rock. She wept for her love. Her tears flowing down washed away the rock, leaving only the arch. Her brave returned and took her away to his home with the sky people."

Lori stared at the rock formation, picturing the beautiful maiden and the brave who rescued her.

"Turn around."

She turned at his bidding.

He held a digital camera. "Smile."

"I don't want my picture taken." But a smile came anyway.

"Too late." He pressed something on the back of the camera. "You want to see?"

She didn't like pictures of herself; all she could see were the hidden scars and pain of the past decade. "No, thanks." She walked to the bicycle and waited for him.

"You aren't mad at me?"

She shook her head. "I don't like to see pictures of myself."

"You look pretty."

She gave him a withering glance. "That's what you want to see." She could see the other 999 words the picture would paint. She pulled the sleeves of the too-big sweatshirt down over her hands and climbed on the front of the bike.

Their next stop was the British landing where Captain Charles Roberts came at night and successfully took Fort Mackinac by surrender. Garth snapped another picture while she read the marker describing the event. They paused again on the west shore to look across the water at the five-mile Mackinac Bridge connecting the two Michigan peninsulas, spanning from Mackinaw City to St. Ignace.

"Can we go across the bridge to St. Ignace?" Lori asked.

Garth was fiddling with his camera again. "Not this trip. There won't be time." He smiled at her. "But we can come back."

"Did you take another picture of me?"

He smiled mischievously and slipped the camera back into his pocket.

Next came Devil's Kitchen, another rock formation gouged out of the cliff side. As soon as he pulled the camera from his pocket, she snatched it from him with a smile. "My turn. You stand over there."

He pressed a button on top of the camera. The lens on the front opened and motored out. He pointed to the view screen on the back. "Look here and press this button." He strode to the concave depression in the cliff and waited with a roguish smile.

She pressed the button but wasn't sure if it took. "How do I look at it?"

Garth came over and turned a knob. The picture she'd taken appeared on the little screen. It was hard to tell if it was good, but Garth said, "You should be a photographer."

"I don't think so."

"A model then."

She let out a rush of breath and placed the camera in his hand.

"No. You should, really," he said. "I'll show you the other pictures."

"I'll pass." She climbed back onto the bike with her hands inside the sweatshirt sleeves.

He climbed on behind her. "They're good. They all have you in them."

"That's why I'll pass."

He directed her to pull over by some trees between the road and the water. He took her hand and pulled her toward a stone marker. "This is where they met."

The marker had a picture of the scene of the first meeting of Richard and Elise, the main characters in *Somewhere in Time*. The movie had piqued her interest in the island, but it was the island itself that was wooing her to love it.

"Would you take our picture?" She heard Garth say and turned around. He stood with a couple who had stopped their bicycles.

The man said, "If you return the favor."

Garth handed the man his camera and came to stand next to her. She looked up at him sideways. He knew she wouldn't protest with others present. *Careful, girl, or you'll lose your heart to him.*

"Okay. Now smile." The man pressed the button. "That should be great."

Garth took their picture next. The couple thanked them and climbed on their bikes and rode away. She and Garth rode in the other direction.

Garth leaned forward near her ear. "See that brick building coming up on the left?"

Beyond the playground equipment a long red-brick building stretched from that road to the one above. She nodded.

"That's the island school. My roommate from college, Will Tobin, teaches there."

That was a school? It looked like a school, but she hadn't thought about people possibly living on the island all year. Why not? A car-less world. It would be a great place to live.

They ended up back in town as Garth said they would, and he gave her directions to the Butterfly House.

☙

The Butterfly House was a converted old house. Garth hadn't been there before. In the lobby Lorelei went straight to the large display window with hundreds of chrysalides hung on stair-step rungs. Were they alive or just a display? Some of the silken cocoons were empty; then he noticed a couple of butterflies hanging onto newly vacated dwellings, drying their wings.

Lorelei drew in a quick breath. "They're real."

From behind them a voice said, "There are actual caterpillar farms."

He and Lorelei turned to the older man behind the counter.

"We get about five hundred chrysalides a week packed in crushproof containers and hang them just like they would be on a tree. Once the butterflies emerge and dry their wings, we put them in the hothouse with the others. They live only about fourteen days."

Garth followed Lorelei over to the counter, and when she gazed up at him he had to catch his breath.

"I want to go in. My treat."

He forced air into his lungs and held up his hand. "I've got it." He pulled out his wallet and paid. They each received a large round butterfly sticker for their shirts that would grant them readmittance as often as they liked that day.

He pulled back the heavy clear plastic strips hanging in the doorway to barricade the delicate insects within. Lorelei stepped inside, and he followed. It was probably a good twenty degrees warmer in there, so he pulled off his sweatshirt and took out his camera in case he could sneak a picture.

They moved along the short meandering path through the bright flowers and green bushes. Time touched nothing inside these walls; it was like an eternal summer. He liked all the seasons, but summer held a special fondness for him; he'd first seen Lorelei in the summer, and she had returned at the end of summer.

He watched her survey the room of fluttering butterflies and snapped a couple of pictures without her knowing. They turned the first corner in the brick path.

Lorelei rushed to a blue metal bench. "Look! It's shaped like a giant butterfly."

He raised his camera, and surprisingly she let him take her picture. They walked past the miniature waterfall fountain, and a butterfly lit on the sticker on Lorelei's sweatshirt. He raised his camera as she turned to look down at the yellow butterfly, but it flew away.

As they wound toward the end and were watching the iridescent blue butterflies fluttering in the corner, a lighter blue butterfly landed on Lorelei's bangs. Garth slowly raised his camera. "Don't move." He snapped the picture as Lorelei was looking up through her bangs at the butterfly; then it flew away.

"Look." She pointed to her pant leg. A brown owl butterfly was holding onto her jeans.

He took another picture, and even when Lorelei walked around, it wouldn't give up its hold.

When they were ready to exit, Garth gently blew on a butterfly that sat on Lorelei's shoulder. It flew away, and Lorelei smiled up at him. The one on her leg would not let go even when she shook her leg repeatedly. Garth found an employee to help because the signs instructed them not to touch the butterflies.

A lanky red-haired man looked at the owl butterfly and said, "Time to get off. These nice people want to leave."

The butterfly didn't move. "I guess he's not listening," Lorelei said.

The guy smacked his forehead with his palm. "I forgot. They don't have ears." He pinched the butterfly between the lengths of his index and middle fingers and plucked it off then walked away.

Garth held back the plastic in the doorway at the other end of the path for Lorelei. They both stepped into the mirror room where they looked at all sides of themselves for stowaways.

In the gift shop Lorelei bought a fuzzy pen with a butterfly on the end. They collected their tandem bike and rode back to the shop to return it.

"I can't wait any longer. I want to go into some shops." She headed for the nearest one.

Whatever the lady wanted. He followed behind. Everything about Mackinac was new to him through the delight of Lorelei's eyes. He had visited the island so often, sometimes up to six times a summer, that the trips offered little that was fresh; but today was different.

He took her hand in his. She soon slipped her hand free to look at knickknacks. He watched as her face lit up with each new find. She settled on a mug with lilacs printed all the way around it and a *Somewhere in Time* sweatshirt. Though he offered to put her purchase in his backpack, she insisted on carrying it—in the hand between them. As she looked into another shop window to watch a confectioner cool fudge on a large marble table, he slipped around behind her and took her free hand. She seemed to be mesmerized by the process. The hot fudge was poured out onto a large marble table and worked into a long loaf-type shape down the center of the table until it cooled.

"This is my treat." She went to the door.

He released her hand to open the door for her. She picked a traditional chocolate fudge, his favorite; a caramel-colored maple walnut fudge, another favorite; and a cherry almond fudge. Neapolitan in a little pink box.

Back on the sidewalk she held a bag now in each hand.

"I can put those in my backpack." That was, after all, the idea for bringing it.

"These aren't heavy."

He guessed that ruled out holding her hand. She was like a butterfly at rest; if he moved too fast, she would flutter away. What would she do if he acted on his daydream and took her in his arms and swung her around? He would caress back a stray lock and study every inch of her face. Then he would bend slowly to her waiting lips and give her a sweet, tender kiss.

She turned from the shop window she had been perusing and looked up at him. This was his opportunity. He could kiss her now, except for the slight pull of her eyebrows. Maybe he could kiss her concerns away.

She looked away. "I'm hungry."

Even now he could reach out and run his fingers through her soft, silky hair. He had imagined how it felt a hundred times. The island could be a romantic place, but not for them, not today. Too bad. "There's a restaurant across the street that looks good."

❧

After lunch Lori took out the fudge, and they had a taste of each. Smooth and creamy.

The island seemed magical. Tranquil. No cars—just the *clip-clop* of horses walking by. She talked Garth into a few extra shops before they took a carriage tour to see more of the attractions. Their friendly guide, Haley, related information about the sights and stories of the people along with some history and even told a few island jokes. By the time the tour was over, the cloudy sky had broken forth with a light shower.

It wasn't until she descended from the surrey that she realized her hip had been telling her it was going to rain. She had so enjoyed herself that she had forgotten about her bum hip. The pain bloomed all at once, nearly taking away her breath. She hobbled over next to the storefront under the awning out of the rain.

"You're limping. Are you okay?" The concern in his voice was etched on his face, as well.

"I'm fine. I have a bad hip—the remains of the car accident

I was in back in high school. I'll be fine as soon as I take my medication." She unzipped her waist pack and rooted around inside. Her little pillbox wasn't there. "I forgot it!" She had changed clothes so many times that morning she had forgotten to pick it up from the counter.

"What is it?"

"It's for inflammation."

"I have something that might help." He dropped his pack to the ground and pulled out a small first-aid kit. Like a Boy Scout he was prepared. She knew over-the-counter pills wouldn't work as well as her prescription, but at least they would ease her discomfort so she could enjoy the rest of the day.

The wind rustled the fabric awning, protecting them from the rain, and blew a strand of hair across Lori's face. As Garth brushed back the stray tendril, their gazes locked, and an indiscernible feeling passed between them. It was the same look he'd given her before she distracted him with lunch. She broke the trance before his blue gaze sucked her in.

They strolled past several shops before they entered the Island Bookstore. She bought three books on local history and a video of *Somewhere in Time*. She also purchased four novels, three of which took place on the island and one that had inspired the movie. In another shop she found a teapot that nearly matched her new lilac mug.

On the whole, she had enjoyed the day tremendously, but it was time for her to leave this dream spot. Her hip hurt more than before, so they took an earlier ferry than originally planned.

The ride was quiet as Lori dealt with the constant ache, an ever-present reminder of all she had lost. Garth kept glancing over at her, concerned. She suspected he drove faster than he should because of it.

৯

Garth parked in the driveway of her cottage and came around the truck to help her out, hooking his arm around her waist to support her. When she winced at each step, he decided, like it or not, to scoop her up in his arms. She didn't resist and surprised him by resting her head on his shoulder.

"I'm sorry to be a bother to you."

"You're no bother." He set her gently on the couch and got her medication and a glass of milk. "Is there anything else I can do for you?"

"I'll be fine. I'm going to bed, and in the morning I'll be as good as new."

He wondered about that and sat on the edge of the couch for a few minutes longer. Was she really all right? She had been in such pain. "If you're sure you're okay, I'll go bring in your stuff."

"I'm fine. Thank you." She reached out and touched his arm. "Oh, Garth, I had a nice time today."

He smiled back at her. "So did I."

He returned a few minutes later with her bags of treasures and placed them on the table, adding his two sweaters. She needed them more than he did, and he had plenty of others.

Her eyes were closed, and she was lying so still. He crossed the room to the couch and noticed her even breathing. Could she be asleep so fast? He spread the blue-and-white-striped afghan from the back of the couch over her. She didn't move. He brushed a strand of hair from her face and lightly kissed her brow.

She stirred then with a soft purr like a contented kitten. "Please, Lord, let me live on Mackinac Island."

Did she mean to say that aloud? He studied her face. Or was she speaking her desires in her sleep?

He tiptoed out and locked the door behind him. He had never considered living on the island, but it would be a nice place to call home. He climbed in his SUV and drove to his cottage. He hadn't planned to live in his parents' place forever. Maybe it was time for a change.

He hooked the cord from his digital camera to the front of his computer. Soon the pictures of Lorelei he'd taken were before him. Was Mackinac the change he needed? He clicked on each picture one by one to enlarge them. It had been a good day for them with the exception of Lorelei's hip hurting her. He'd wished he could take her pain upon himself, but he could only watch her suffer.

He clicked on the first picture of him and Lorelei at the *Somewhere in Time* marker. Apparently the man had taken a picture before Lorelei was facing the camera. Her head was cocked sideways looking up at him with that same disbelieving, impish look she had when he was trying to sell her on the fairy story at the fire. He clicked on the next picture of them by the marker. They looked like a regular happy couple. He would make this one into an eight-by-ten.

How did one go about living on Mackinac Island? He looked at his watch as he headed for the kitchen. It wasn't too late to call. He opened his address book and dialed.

"Yo," came a voice over the line.

"Will? This is Garth."

"Hey, roomie. It's been awhile. What's up?"

Whenever he talked to Will, it was as if no time had passed. "I was on the island today and was thinking about you."

"It's pretty late in the season for you to come here."

"There's this gal—" He could feel a smile pull at his mouth.

"Say no more."

"I would have called you, but I didn't have your number with me. I wish I could have introduced you to her."

"So you called to say I missed an opportunity to meet your girlfriend?"

"Not exactly." He would skip the part about Lorelei not being his girlfriend yet. "I was wondering how hard it would be for a guy like me to get a job on the island."

Will made a noise halfway between a chuckle and a snort.

"I'm not talking about the school. Those jobs are probably sealed tight. But is there anything else you think I could do?"

"You aren't quitting teaching, are you?"

He turned and leaned against the counter. "No, but I figure a teaching job on the island would be impossible. If something comes up, would you let me know?"

"You're serious."

He ran a hand through his hair. "I don't know if I am or not. I'm just knocking around some ideas. I'll probably end up living the rest of my life in my parents' cottage. I should consider buying it from them."

"Well, this past Wednesday my teaching partner was in a bad mood, snapping at everyone, so I gave her a wide path all day."

Why was Will telling him about his frustrations with his coworker?

"Then on Thursday she came in giddy and weird. I wasn't sure if I should ask her what was up. Didn't need to. She blurted out that she was pregnant. She and her husband have been trying for years."

Garth pushed away from the counter. "And she's not coming back."

"You're ruining my story."

"Sorry."

"You're about as sorry as a cat in a barrel of mice. She hasn't told the school yet; I'm one of the privileged few who know. She's waiting until she's further along before announcing it—to make sure she doesn't lose the baby. So don't go calling the school asking about her position. Send me your resumé, and when the job is officially open, I'll submit it."

"What do you think my chances would be?" He twisted the phone cord around his hand.

"I'll give you my endorsement and talk you up. Since I know you, that might weigh heavily with the hiring board. It's no guarantee, but I'd say your chances are pretty good."

After they talked awhile longer, Garth hung up. His chances would be good. Is that what he wanted? He glanced around the main living area. He was comfortable here, but was he supposed to stay here? *Lord, is this an open door? Show me what to do. Where do You want me to be?*

eight

Tuesday afternoon Garth knocked on Lorelei's door a little louder but still no answer. He tapped the small photo book he had bought in town on his palm. It had a picture of a sunset over water on it and was perfect for the Mackinac pictures he had printed for her.

Her purple grape was parked in the driveway so she couldn't have gone far—maybe for a walk or down on the beach. He walked around to the back of the building and past the deck. She sat at the picnic table staring out across the lake with her notebook open in front of her.

"Howdy, neighbor," he called as he approached. "I have something for you."

He noticed her stiffen and quickly wipe her face with her hands before turning to greet him with a forced smile. His own smile slipped to concern. Her eyes were red and puffy. He hurried his last few steps.

"Are you all right?" He straddled the bench next to her, putting the photo album with her notebook.

"I'm fine." She tried to cover the fact she had been crying.

"You've been crying." Tenderness softened his voice.

Her smile melted as she turned from him and gazed back out at the lake. He glanced at the display of fall colors on the opposite shore, but he guessed she saw none of it—the clear still water, the brilliant color-laden trees, the awe-inspiring beauty. She was struggling inside and losing the battle. A tear trickled down her cheek. She covered her face with her hands to conceal her anguish.

He had the urge to wrap his arms around her, but if she wouldn't admit there was a problem she wouldn't be comforted either.

"What's wrong?" He reached out his hand to her but stopped when she shook her head. Remembering what she'd said the night of the beach fire about being alone, he thought it best to leave her to herself.

"I want you to know if you need a shoulder to cry on or an ear to listen, I have two of each."

No response.

"You know how to reach me if you need me, any time of the day or night." He couldn't tell if she heard him. "I won't bother you any longer. I'm just a phone call away or a good loud holler." He hoped to get some kind of reaction from her.

Nothing.

He hated to leave but didn't know what else she would let him do for her, so he started to stand. He was still straddling the bench when she covered his hand on the table with hers, wet with tears. She didn't say a word. He stared at their hands for a moment then sat back down. Though she wasn't ready to talk, she obviously didn't want to be alone, and he certainly didn't want to leave her so upset.

He didn't know how long they sat there in silence before she lifted her head and stared across the lake. Finally she spoke. "Doug would have loved it here," she said softly. "He loved the outdoors. . .and the changing seasons. Florida drove him nuts." She gave a little laugh void of humor. "He said they only had two seasons, summer and hurricane."

He could see her struggle against tears again; her bottom lip quivered. "It's not fair. He shouldn't have died." The tears came unhindered now.

He didn't know if she would let him comfort her, but he scooted closer and tentatively wrapped his arm around her slender shoulders. "It's going to be okay."

"I wish he were here." She fell into his waiting embrace with sobs.

What manner of man was this Doug to captivate her heart? A boyfriend, fiancé, or maybe—her husband? He had felt something stood between them, holding her back. Was this it? Was it Doug? Even in death he held what Garth longed for—her heart.

A wave of jealousy drove through him. He knew if Doug were here with her Garth most likely would not be the one sitting next to her. He was suddenly disgusted with himself. The poor man was dead, and all he could think of was himself.

She continued to sob gently in his arms as he caressed her hair away from her face. He knew sometimes a person just needed to cry. It was part of the healing process, cleansing the soul.

After a few minutes her crying subsided. She pulled back and wiped her face then turned to him. "I'm sorry I got your shirt all wet." She wiped the front of him.

He grabbed her hands in his to stop their nervous motion. "It's all right. The shirt's washable."

She smiled at that and dropped her hands. He released them, letting her take them back. "I'm sorry. I thought I was over the crying part. I try to put it behind me and go on with my life. I guess I can't see the future without him and Aunt Lillah. They were my whole life, as pathetic as it was. So I keep returning to the past that always ends in their tragic deaths."

"Tell me about it."

She looked a little surprised at his quiet request but began to tell of the house fire that had swept through the two-story building in a matter of minutes. "Doug woke me from a deep sleep and carried me out of the house. He went back for Aunt Lillah but was overtaken by the smoke. Firefighters carried them both out, but it was too late." She choked on her last words.

Doug must have been her husband. So young to be a widow already. Though he didn't want to, he would back off pursuing her and give her some space. He would be the *friend* she needed. "Why did you come up here by yourself?"

She took a deep breath. "Why indeed? Lyell, one of my physical therapists, told me that when the physical pain was too much I needed to find a place in the past that was happy and go there in my mind until I could overcome the pain or until it was finished torturing me." She motioned toward the lake. "I came here. This was one of the last places I can truly remember being happy. The Lord found me here." She took a deep breath as if remembering something.

And Garth had found her here, as well. "Wouldn't that attach a negative emotion to a pleasant memory?"

"Surprisingly not."

"Wouldn't you rather have the comfort and support of your parents and family?"

She paused. "Doug and Aunt Lillah were the last of my family. And, yes, I would rather be with my parents if I could, but they died when I was in high school."

He noted she was more reflective about her parents' death. The pain wasn't fresh. She had healed from that one.

"Mom and Dad let Doug stay home with a couple of his friends, or he would have been killed that night, too."

"The same accident you were in?"

"They say I was lucky. Sometimes I wonder." She shrugged.

Something she said played over in his head. *Mom and Dad let Doug stay home with friends. . .I was in high school.* She wasn't mourning for a husband. Doug was her brother!

In those moments of openness and comfort, they moved from casual friendship to a deeper friendship, more comfortable and with greater understanding.

He reached over and caressed a stray tear away as he listened to her talk more about her family.

Suddenly she flipped her notebook shut and excused herself. Garth wondered if it was their physical proximity that caused her to flee or the emotional closeness. She must have felt it, too. Or was it his longing for them to grow closer that was pulling her into a relationship she might not be ready for?

"I brought these for you." He stood and held out the photo book. "They're of Mackinac."

"Thank you." She took the offered gift and limped away

from him. Once she was out of sight and inside, he sank back down on the bench and rested his forehead on his clasped hands.

Why, Father? Why does she always run away from me? What have I done to scare her? Show me how to help her.

&

Lori watched Garth from the window, careful to remain out of sight should he happen to look in her direction. She longed to go back down to him, but she knew she had to hold tight reins on her heart. She couldn't let go and risk being torn apart again.

He remained at the table a long while with his head bowed, as if in prayer. Was he praying for her?

She splayed her hand on the cold glass and leaned her forehead against it. Garth deserved a whole woman, not someone whose body and spirit were broken and battered.

Lord—

She stood up straight. In that single word that opened her heart in prayer, she knew Garth *was* praying for her.

Please, Lord. . . What should she pray for? *Squelch any feelings he might have for me. Bring the perfect woman into his life.* She choked back a tear, this time not for her recent loss but for something that could never be.

nine

On Thursday Garth's eyes were bright with excitement as he stood in the breezeway outside her door. "How would you like to see the most spectacular light show in the world tonight?"

"What? Like at a planetarium or something?"

"Or something. Are you game?"

"Sure."

"Great. I'll pick you up at one."

Lori's mouth dropped open. "In the morning?" No, he couldn't mean that.

"Mm-hm. Dress warm. I'll see you then."

Later she couldn't decide whether to go to bed early and set her alarm or just stay up. She opted for getting some sleep, but it was a waste of time. She got up at midnight to make a snack and wait.

She jumped at the sudden knock on her door. She had been watching for Garth's vehicle, but obviously he hadn't driven. Where was this light show anyway?

"Here. Use this." He held out a coat. "It's my mother's. She leaves it up here at the cottage. Saturday I'll take you to a place where you can shop for a coat. They have the best wool sweaters, too."

He guided her out onto the deck. She looked up at the diamond-studded sky. It was a beautifully clear night, and the stars were winking at her as though they had a secret. The kind of night made for romance.

She looked up at him sharply. That's not what he was thinking, was it? She swallowed hard when he looked down at her and smiled. "I tho"—she cleared her throat—"I thought we were going to a planetarium or something to see a light show."

He grinned at her. "It's the *or something*. The light show is coming to us."

In the deck light she could see a twinkle in his clear blue eyes. For a moment she lost herself in their depths. She gave herself a mental shake and turned back to the starlit sky.

She faced the rail, looking out toward the lake. He stood with his back to the rail, watching her. His gaze made her nerves tingle. She could easily give her heart to this man, but she couldn't let that happen. "I only see stars. Are these your light show?"

"They're only the prelude. Have you ever heard of the aurora borealis?"

She shook her head.

"Then the aurora borealis, or northern lights, is like nothing you have ever seen. It's a curtain of colored lights rippling across the night sky, shifting and changing as if God Himself were gently blowing on it. A magnificent, heavenly symphony of lights. I like to think of it as a glimpse of heaven. A fraction of what it will be like to stand in the presence of Christ in all His glory."

It was easy to get caught up in his enthusiasm. The picture he painted sounded beautiful, but she couldn't quite imagine it. Was this another one of his stories? "When is this show due to begin?"

"Any minute."

Her breath caught as the sky ignited in a luminescent curtain of wavering colors, just as he'd described it. "It's almost like daylight out here." An interesting quiet swishing, almost a crackle, accompanied the bright glow.

Watching the lights dance and play across the sky and reflect off the water below did indeed remind her of what heaven could be like. She knew Garth was still watching her reaction to the light show, but it didn't bother her now because she was in awe of the spectacular show God was putting on. "What causes it?"

He turned to the sky. "God."

"I know. But how do scientists explain it?"

"I don't like to think about the scientific explanation. It only spoils the effect."

He was probably right.

"Eskimo myth says if you whistle at it, it will swoop down and carry you away."

"Did you ever try?"

He stretched out his arms from his sides. "I'm still here, aren't I?"

They stood in breathtaking admiration for nearly an hour before the aurora scattered and disappeared as quickly as it had come. Neither one spoke for several minutes. Garth finally broke the silence. "It leaves me in awe every time I witness it."

She turned to him. "Thank you for sharing it with me."

"My pleasure."

"I have never seen anything more beautiful."

"I've seen a few things that come close," he said in a husky voice as he gazed at her.

Oh, dear. He's not thinking of kissing me, is he?

He cleared his throat. "I should let you go so you can get some sleep."

&

Lori had been curious when Garth insisted on taking her shopping for some winter sweaters. She couldn't stay much longer in Michigan without warmer clothes. He knew of the best place in the area but refused to give her directions. He would drive her. Her curiosity was piqued even further now that Kalkaska lay ten miles behind them. If this place wasn't in Kalkaska, then where? "Where are you taking me?"

"You'll see. I promise you'll love it." He beamed like a little boy taking her to his found treasure.

"How far away is this place?"

"A ways."

She huffed. "How long will it take to get there?"

"Awhile."

He wasn't giving anything away, but she could pester him.

"I know. You aren't taking me to buy anything. You're kidnapping me."

"There's an idea," he said with a smile, arching his eyebrows.

"You're out of luck. There's no one to pay the ransom."

"You'll have to pay your own ransom, I guess."

"How can I do that if you're holding me hostage?"

"Then I guess I get to keep you." He reached over and rested his hand on her arm.

Lori's stomach did a little flip at his touch. She hastily folded her arms in her lap, forcing him to pull back his hand. "Are we there yet?" she said in her best little-kid whine.

He laughed aloud.

Finally they pulled into a seaside town called Traverse City. The trees opened up to reveal the expanse of the blue green water. Not actually seaside, but more like bayside. Grand Traverse Bay off Lake Michigan, to be exact. Sailboats dotted the sparkling water.

"Here we are, my beautiful hostage." Garth pulled up to an unimpressive rustic log building. Was this one of those outdoorsy kinds of stores? The sign on the front read: TRAVERSE BAY WOOLEN COMPANY.

Lori stepped inside the weathered interior and stopped short, doubtful she would find anything to her liking in this backwoods place. She scanned the log furnishings until her gaze landed on a deer-antler lamp.

The place reminded her of a camping store, though she didn't see any equipment for that. She half-expected to see woodland critters poking their furry heads out to view the strange Floridian who had invaded their turf. But there were none, only statuaries of small animals.

This was what all the secrecy was about? This was his treasure?

She wanted to turn and walk out, but Garth's eyebrows bobbing up and down demanded her opinion.

"It's nice." She forced a smile and hoped a mall was nearby.

"Come on. Give it a chance." He took her by the hand and

pulled her through the store. "My mom and sisters love this place."

As they made their way deeper in, Lori discovered it was rich in character and charm. At a glance the clothing ranged from Native American to classic, casual to dressy.

Garth perused a stack of sweaters. "Here's one." He immediately put it back. "No, this one." He held up a beautiful hand-knit sweater with an entire scene on it; a lofty evergreen tree, a snow-capped mountain, and a sparkling stream.

"It's gorgeous." She took it from him.

His smile broadened at her change of heart toward the store.

By lunchtime she had tried on more than a dozen sweaters and picked her four favorites. Next she selected a long, tan wool coat and a scarf with a beret. She tried them on and turned around for his opinion. He was close by, watching her, and gave his approval. He liked everything she chose.

"So do I have everything I need?"

He smiled and held up his fingers.

She tucked her hands in the pockets of the coat to show him she didn't need gloves. He chuckled and chose a pair that matched the scarf and beret. She slipped them on, completing the ensemble, and struck a modeling pose.

"Perfect," he said softly with a nod.

An odd feeling ran through her under his intense gaze, and heat spread across her cheeks. She removed the coat and other items and nervously fingered the sweaters. "I don't know which one to put back."

"Why do you have to put any back?" He came up beside her.

"I don't need all four. I probably don't even need three, but I don't think I could choose two to give up."

"I'll buy one for you."

She looked up at him sharply. "No, you won't."

His expression changed to something akin to disappointment. She felt bad for snapping at him. "You weren't serious?"

"Naw." He shook his head, but the hurt remained in his eyes.

ten

Lori stepped out onto the deck with her hot cup of tea and took the chair opposite Josie. A colorful windsock twirled in the cool fall breeze. A few leaves still clung to the trees.

"It sounds as if things are getting serious between the two of you," Josie said.

"We're just friends," Lori snapped and scalded her lips on the edge of her tea mug.

Josie had come up by herself for a long weekend, no doubt to check up on her and make sure she wasn't wallowing in grief. Lori had looked forward to her visit; but if this was the bent the conversation would keep taking, she wasn't so sure she could put up with it all weekend.

"Just friends?" Josie's brown eyes rounded.

"Yes. Just friends."

"Let's see—he takes you to church and out to eat twice a week."

"It makes sense to eat in town while we're there." She sounded defensive, even to herself.

Josie snorted. "How many times a week does he eat dinner over here? Four? Five? That takes care of the week."

"Only once or twice," she said, although the past two weeks it had been three. "It's not as if it's planned. He comes by to check on things. I think your father asked him to. I appreciate his looking out for. . .things, so I offer him dinner."

"Which he would never turn down. Not planned, ha." She leaned forward and looked at Lori. "He just *happens* to stop by at dinnertime. And you just *happen* to have enough food for two. I would say something is planned whether you want to admit it or not."

Planned—no. She hadn't planned anything. True, she did make extra—just in case. He's a bachelor; he didn't get home-cooked meals. She was only trying to help—a friend. Yes, that was it. Help a friend. He'd been so nice to check up on her to make sure everything was working fine and she was safe. She knew why he did it. Mr. Davenport had asked him to. She was sure of it. And she did so like having a friend up here. She just had to be careful to keep things as friends.

"Then you made that trip to Mackinac Island—now there's a romantic place."

Lori opened her mouth to protest, but Josie went on.

"Don't even think about denying it. I saw the pictures. Trips into Mancelona and Kalkaska, even Traverse City last weekend, and the Dunes—"

"The Sand Dunes was Gretchen's idea." She spoke up quickly, pointing a finger in the air. Why had she opened her big mouth and told Josie all the wonderful places she had been? She'd thought it would reassure Josie she was fine. Now she realized her mistake.

Josie rolled her eyes. "If he wanted to get out of it, which obviously he didn't, I'm sure a smart guy like him could have come up with a plausible excuse." She leaned back in her chair and put her hand to her chin. "What else? Oh, yeah, the aurora borealis. A rendezvous under the romantic northern lights." She moved her eyebrows up and down.

She hadn't told Josie she saw it with Garth. She had purposely left him out of it.

"Maybe you two were too busy to pay attention to the sky. Perhaps gazing into each other's eyes."

Garth had been staring at her at the beginning of the light show. That was only to see her reaction to the lights; he was so excited about them. "He's a science teacher. It was a science thing. Nothing more."

"A science thing? Ha!" She turned and looked with pleading in her brown eyes. "Lori, maybe you're not interested in Garth—though I think you are—but he is obviously interested in you. Don't string him along. Garth Kessel is a great guy. He's drop-dead gorgeous, especially his eyes. He's a Christian, kind, considerate, and *very* patient."

She already knew all that. "I'm not interested in a relationship right now."

Josie's smile widened.

"What?" Lori said.

"I noticed you didn't say you weren't interested in Garth."

Lori gave a heavy sigh. "I just can't right now."

She was interested. She just wasn't willing to risk it.

☙

After her talk with Josie, Lori thought a lot about her relationship with Garth. No, not relationship—friendship. Maybe he wasn't being kind out of some sense of duty. She had to put a stop to his growing affections.

Lori's head sank into her pillow; two nights of tossing and turning were enough. She would sleep tonight even if the nightmare came; she longed for sleep.

"There's nothing between us," she heard herself telling Josie. "We're just friends."

"Nothing, ha! How long are you going to fool yourself?"

She wasn't fooling herself. She treasured Garth's friendship. He was kind and patient and caring when she needed him. Always there to comfort her and lend a helping hand. But he wouldn't always be there, and that was the problem.

She recalled the warmth of his embrace when she sat by the lake and cried for Doug. And his attentiveness to show her all of Mackinac Island he could in a single day, though he had seen it more than a dozen times. The concern in his eyes when her hip caused her great pain. She smiled at his little-boy pleasure in sharing his treasured Traverse Bay Woolen Company.

Yes, she had suspected his feelings went beyond friendship, but she hadn't encouraged it. She just needed a friend, and Garth was eager to be there for her. It was nice not to be so alone. Okay, so she was fooling herself.

Maybe she hadn't encouraged Garth, but she certainly

hadn't discouraged him either.

On Monday he stopped by to check on the firewood supply he knew she never used. She realized Josie was right then, and his excuses for dropping by were just that—excuses.

"I thought maybe you and Josie built a fire while she was here." He stood in the breezeway outside the door, looking past her into the cottage.

She didn't invite him in as she normally did. "We decided not to bother with one. I'm sorry you troubled yourself."

"It's no trouble. You know I like to help."

A little too much for your own good. "Everything is working fine, so no help is needed."

He ignored her subtle dismissal but seemed as uncomfortable as she felt. "I was thinking of ordering a pizza or going into town for a burger. Do you want to join me?"

Yes, she wanted to but wouldn't. "I ate a little while ago."

"How about dessert? I'll buy you an ice cream cone." Hope mingled with the hurt in his eyes.

"I don't feel like ice cream. I was going to try to finish my book." She held up the volume with her finger marking the place. That was lame.

"Okay." The dejected sound in his voice and the droop of his mouth pressed at her heart.

"If everything is fine here, then I'll be on my way."

"Everything is fine and dandy," she said with an extra dose of cheerfulness that was far from the agony she was suffering. When he left, a void ripped open inside her.

From the back window that faced the beach she watched him go. Shoulders slumped and head down, he kicked his way across the sand and up the rise to his place.

She felt sick to her stomach and wished she hadn't forced down that sandwich before his arrival.

He looked so hurt. Wasn't that the point? He would be better off without her in the long run. So why was she so miserable? She hurled her book across the room, plopped down on the sofa, and cried into her hands.

≈

Garth stretched out on the couch. So Miss Lorelei Hayes had tired of his company. He'd hoped for so much more. The only woman he had the slightest interest in, and she'd brushed him off.

What went wrong? What had *he* done wrong?

Surely he could do something to change her mind. Hadn't she enjoyed his company? Why invite him in for dinner so often—at all—if not?

Had Josie said something against him to her? Why would she do that? She wouldn't, would she?

Maybe Lorelei needed a little space. Was he crowding her by going over so often?

He lay there in his confusion well after dark. "I suppose I should get something to eat." He pulled himself off the couch and walked to the refrigerator. Lorelei wasn't going to offer her company. He missed her; he hadn't seen her all weekend with Josie visiting, and here it was Monday night and still no sunshine from her smiling face.

He rooted around inside the refrigerator then kicked the door shut. He wasn't hungry anyway. He walked outside and looked over at Lorelei's place. *What did I do wrong, Lord? I want to fix this, but I don't know how.* She said she came up here to be alone. He certainly hadn't afforded her that. He would give her time. But not too much.

≈

On Wednesday when they went to church, Garth was standoffish, polite, and cordial but remained at arm's length where she had pushed him. He didn't come around on Thursday or Friday. She realized how much time they'd spent together and missed his company. . .his friendship. . .their relationship. Her promise to herself not to become involved shattered.

Would he ever come back, or had she scared him off completely? That was her intent, but now she wished she hadn't.

On Saturday she sat outside with her notebook at the

picnic table in her new coat. She hoped being outside would be less threatening. He said he could see her from his place.

She picked up her pen and tapped it on her lips.

The last leaves clung to the late fall branches.

She didn't like the line and crossed it out.

The diamond-sparkled lake rippled in the wind.

She scribbled it out faster than she wrote it.

The trees rustling in the gentle br—
No!

Again she rejected the words. She glanced toward Garth's place. *Where are you?* She put her pen back on the paper.

The girl, sitting on the stupid bench in the stupid cold feeling very stupid.

She studied the page. *I'll title it "The Stupid Poem."*

She pushed the notebook away from her and rested her arms on the wood table. Who was she trying to fool? She couldn't write poetry, nor did she want to. The only poetry she could write was the roses-are-red kind.

She pulled her notebook back toward her and tapped the pen on the paper, then wrote, *Roses are red. Violets are blue. Garth is so wonderful. Why would he like you?*

She turned to a new page.

I'm so confused. Here I sit, waiting for a man who will not come. A man I pushed away. I like Garth. He's a wonderful man. I like him a lot. But what happens when he finds out I'm not perfect? My. . .defects?

I am afraid of my growing feelings for him. And I am afraid of not feeling at all. Sinking ever so slowly into that dark pit void of emotions. It's lonely down there. I know. I visited once and don't care to return. I feel fragile and vulnerable. I don't know if I could handle it very well if things didn't work out between us.

So here I sit. . .waiting. . .debating. . .out in the cold on a hard bench with my hip aching. I'm such an emotional mess. I don't even know what I want. Should I just go back inside and leave well enough alone? But I can't. I hurt him. I can't leave things this way. If he doesn't appear soon, I'll go over and talk to him. No, I'll call him. But what would I say? I can't think of one intelligent thing to say. What's the use? He probably thinks I'm a flaky dimwit and is glad to be rid of me.

I think I want another chance, but I'm afraid to ask. What if I make a mess of it again?

She looked up and was startled to see Garth ambling over with his hands shoved deep in his coat pockets.

She sighed. *Thank You, Lord.*

She closed her journal.

"Howdy. I was going for a walk and saw you out here. Would you like to come along?" He looked tired. Had he gotten as little sleep as she the past week?

She could hear the tentativeness in his voice and chose her words carefully. "I'd love to, but my hip's acting up. I was about to head inside." He looked disappointed. The truth of it was her hip hadn't just started hurting. Between the hard bench and the cold air she'd had an hour of pain now. She had given up on him when he finally showed up. "I was going to make a cup of hot chocolate. Would you like some?"

His demeanor brightened. "Sure. Maybe we could walk later."

She gasped at the pain that shot through her hip when she rose. Garth hooked an arm around her waist to support her. "Are you all right?"

"That bench is harder than I thought," she said through clenched teeth, trying to breathe normally. "I'll be okay once I get the stiffness worked out."

"You shouldn't sit out in the cold so long." She saw compassion on his face and heard it in his words.

"I know." *I was waiting for you, you big lug. If you had come out sooner, I wouldn't have sat so long.* How did he know she was out here very long? Had he been watching her? She could never tell; his place was shrouded in the shadows. She supported herself on him. "If you don't mind, I could use a little help."

She winced with her first hobbled step and was immediately swept up in his strong arms. She didn't protest; instead she slipped her arms around his neck. She was tempted to rest her head on his shoulder but decided against it.

He insisted on getting the cocoa while she reclined on the couch. He knew where things were in this house almost as well as she did. That told her something. He *had* been over a lot.

"Thank you." She took the steaming cup of chocolate. "Not just for this but for helping me. All your help."

"You're more than welcome. I'd help more if I didn't think I was making a pest of myself."

Was there more meaning behind his words than was on the surface? "You're a lot of things, but pest is not one of them."

"I just thought after Monday. . ." He quirked his mouth up on one side.

"I'm sorry about that. I was in a weird mood. I wasn't very good company, even for myself. If I could have gone someplace without me, I would have."

He relaxed a little, and the doldrums surrounding him seemed to dissipate.

They spent the whole unplanned day together, laughing and talking, had lunch at the burger joint, and ordered out pizza for dinner. Had he missed her half as much as she'd missed him?

eleven

The following week they spent every unplanned evening together except Friday, that one they planned. He had asked her Monday if she would like to go to the homecoming football game.

"I haven't been to a homecoming game in years. As a matter of fact, any football game."

"Then it's high time you went."

Lori enjoyed the game. Between the first and second quarters Garth led her over to the snack shack. The score was seven to zero in favor of Garth's school. Before they reached the concession stand, a husky boy with dark hair and dark eyes waylaid them. He looked as if he could be a football player.

"Hey, Mr. Kessel."

"Tyler, how's it going?" Garth shook the boy's hand. "How's college life?"

"Great! I made second string, but the coach still has me play a lot."

"Lori, this is Tyler Jenkins. He was our star fullback for four years straight and has quite an aptitude for science."

"Ty, this is Miss Hayes."

"Hi." Tyler dipped his head shyly.

Garth and Tyler talked for several minutes longer. While they spoke, two blond girls came up and stood on the other side of Garth from her. Garth took a step closer to her and put his hand lightly at the small of her back, not hesitating in his dialogue with Tyler.

"Hello, Mr. Kessel," the taller of the two girls said at an opportune break in the conversation.

"Amanda, Ami," Garth said tightly. "This is Miss Hayes."

Lori said hello, but Amanda didn't so much as bat an

eyelash in her direction, while the shorter girl offered no more than a quick sideways glance. Lori looked up at Garth. Was he blushing? She couldn't quite tell in the shadows of the field lights.

"I'm sorry I missed the test yesterday. I was ill, and my mother still kept me home this morning just to be sure," Amanda said with a little smile.

"I'm glad to see you're feeling better. You can make it up on Monday."

"With you after school?" She sounded so innocent.

The color in Garth's face deepened, and he slipped his hand more fully around Lori's waist. "I'll make arrangements for you to take your test in the front office, so you won't be disturbed."

Amanda sighed. "Okay."

"I'll catch you later, Mr. Kessel." Tyler turned to leave.

Amanda smiled at Garth before she headed after Tyler. "Wait up, Ty."

Lori had known girls like that in high school before she had to quit. They wanted attention by causing trouble. She could tell Garth was uneasy, probably trying to figure out what to say after Amanda's display.

She drew in a deep breath. "Mmm—that popcorn sure smells good. I'm hungry."

"Then I shall feed you, m'lady. I can't have you fainting dead away on me for lack of food."

He relaxed a little and even jumped up and cheered, "Go, Blazers!" as the game progressed, then joined the wave when it swept their section.

The Blue Blazers won the game forty-seven to seven, a victorious homecoming.

Later, when Garth took her home, he said, "I'm sorry about Amanda and Ami."

With all the excitement Lori had forgotten the blonds.

"You and Doris were—right—about the girls and the science thing." The admission seemed difficult for him.

"We all have our blind spots." She'd enjoyed seeing Garth

turn three shades of red.

"I was wondering if you would do me a huge favor?" He fidgeted with her hand. "I'm one of the chaperones for the homecoming dance tomorrow night. If you were to go with me, the—students wouldn't—you know—bother me as much." He looked down at her, pleading for rescue.

"You mean the girls flirting with you." She was hard-pressed to contain her smile.

"Yes, the girls."

"Let me see if I have this right? You want to *use* me to fend off the swarm of adolescent girls?"

He dropped his head, his chin resting on his chest. "Yes." After a brief pause he looked back up at her. "Would you do it? I'll be forever in your debt."

"Sure, I'll save you from the Garth-hungry pubescent she-wolves."

"Thank you. I owe you big-time." He gave her a peck on the cheek before bounding out to his vehicle.

His quick kiss on the cheek sent a thrill through her. It confused her, too. She liked it, but it caused her stomach to knot. She knew it was like a green light—okay, move forward. She should put an end to it but didn't want to push him away again. She didn't know what she wanted. Yes, she did. She wanted the impossible.

⋙

She wasn't sure what one wore to a high school dance. She had an idea what the girls might be wearing or what she might have worn ten years ago. But what did an adult wear? A chaperone?

She selected her nicest church dress and fussed a little extra with her hair. She wished it would grow faster. It had been short since the accident, easier for others to take care of until she could do it herself. Then having her hair cut was part of the routine; but now she was growing it out as she had once had it. One more thing robbed from her in that flash of an instant that had changed her life forever. The approving smile Garth gave when he gazed at her caused her heart to race. He'd even bought her a corsage.

The music at the dance was loud. A few songs grated on her nerves, but most were tolerable, and a handful were pleasant.

Afterward, back at her place, he came in and closed the door behind him. "I really appreciate your coming with me tonight." He helped her out of her coat and hung it over the back of a chair.

"I had fun. Thank you for inviting me."

He put his coat over the chair, as well, then stood in front of her with his arms out from his sides. "Name your price. Not that I could ever repay this debt."

"You don't owe me a thing, Garth. You've always been so helpful. I was happy to help you for a change. It makes me not feel quite so much the leech." And she wanted to spend time with him. . .a lot of time.

He rubbed his hands on her upper arms. "You're the prettiest leech I've ever seen."

Her pulse quickened, and she could scarcely take a breath. "Would you like some cocoa or tea?"

"No, thank you."

Now what? They stood face-to-face. Words didn't seem appropriate. Her insides started to swirl under his hypnotic gaze.

He reached out and fingered a loose tendril of hair. "It's so silky. The color so extraordinary." His gaze shifted to her face, studying it, as well.

She swallowed.

"May I kiss you?"

It was gallant of him to ask. "You have before." She touched her cheek where he had given her a parting kiss. But what he asked now was different.

He caressed her cheek where she had touched it. "Not here." He put his index finger lightly to her lips. "Here."

A sudden thrill went through her. *You have kissed me there before. Don't you remember, Bandit?* She nodded her consent.

He lowered his lips to hers in a gentle, lingering kiss. She didn't realize how much she had longed for him to kiss her, and she slipped her arms around his neck. He embraced her with his strong, secure arms and kissed her again.

He pulled away. Neither one spoke as they gazed at each other in silence.

Finally Garth took his coat from the back of the chair and swung it on. "I should go."

Something inside her didn't want him to go. "What about a good-night kiss?"

A shy smile played at the corners of his lips. "I think I already did that."

"May I give you a good-night kiss then?" She felt her face flush. Never in her life had she been so bold. When had she had the chance?

His smile spread across his face and his eyes brightened. "I'd like that." His soft answer made her heart beat faster.

She stepped forward and rested her hands on his strong, broad shoulders, then gave him a tender kiss.

For a moment neither said anything. Then he caressed her cheek with the back of his hand. "Well, good night then," he said but stayed a moment longer.

When he left, she hurried to the kitchen window and watched him until his vehicle disappeared up the steep drive. She spun around in circles. Love was grand. Not even the knowledge things wouldn't last could spoil this moment. She wouldn't let it.

೭

How could he have been so carried away? He had almost told her. Just before he kissed her, the words *I love you* nearly spilled from his lips. He couldn't expect her to feel the same way he did. He'd had ten years to nurture his feelings toward her. She'd had only a couple of months.

He supposed it was partially fear that drove him. Fear of losing her. Gretchen had said Lorelei was staying anywhere from a few weeks to two months. Those two months were up. Would she be leaving soon? She hadn't said anything.

The agony of not knowing when she would walk out of his life again had driven his actions all week, trying to squeeze in every minute he could with her. He had to know. He would ask her casually on the way to church tomorrow.

But he didn't. Church came and went, and he still didn't know the answer to his burning question. He had convinced her to go to lunch with some friends just to be with her. They didn't arrive back at the lake until midafternoon. Now he was at her door, trying to find a tactful way to ask her how long she planned to remain at the lake.

"Do you have plans for dinner?" He knew he was stalling.

She hesitated. "Well. . .not really."

"What does *not really* mean? Either you do or you don't." That sounded a bit curt. He hoped she hadn't noticed, but he was afraid she would say she had a lot of packing to do for her trip.

"I plan to eat something for dinner, but exactly what I don't know until I rummage through the leftovers in the fridge." She cocked her head slightly to one side. "Are you fishing for a home-cooked meal?"

"No." A brilliant idea popped into his head. "Could I cook for you for a change?"

"You cook?"

"Yes, I cook. I'm a bachelor, living alone. It's a matter of survival. My other two options were not very appealing."

"What were they, TV dinners and mac and cheese?"

He grimaced at the thought. "Spending all my money to support the local restaurants or starve."

She became serious. "Yes." But he guessed she was feigning the serious part.

"Yes, what? Yes, I should support the restaurants, or, yes, I should starve?"

"Yes, thank you. I would like to sample your cooking this evening," she said with an impish grin. "But I can't stay long."

This was it. She would tell him she was leaving in the morning.

"Two late nights in a row have left me tired. I need to get to bed early."

"Does Cinderella turn into a pumpkin?" he said with a smile, trying to ease the knot in his stomach with some humor.

"Something like that."

"Then I promise to have the lady home early." He made a sweeping bow.

"Thank you, kind sir," she said with a dip of her head.

"I'll pick you up at five."

He left and headed straight for town to buy what he needed for his food creation, all the while chiding himself for being a coward. Tonight. He would ask her tonight how much longer she was staying at the Davenports' cottage. How much longer would he have to gaze into her emerald green eyes and touch her silken red hair?

If she was staying longer, that was a good sign. Wasn't it? At least he wouldn't have scared her off. But it didn't mean she would be staying because of him. First he had to know if she was even staying.

❧

"Are you staying?" he blurted out.

She looked at him. Hadn't he invited her over? "Well, I thought I'd stay until eight, but I can leave now."

He laid a gentle hand on her arm. "What I meant to say is—will you still need a ride to church next Sunday?"

"I can drive myself, if there's a problem with that."

"Then you are going?" He sounded hopeful.

His sudden odd behavior confused her "I was planning on it unless there is a problem with that, too."

"No, there's no problem with your going, only in your leaving." He sounded wistful. "I would be more than happy to take you to church."

His signals were so erratic she couldn't tell if he was brushing her off or not. At the very least, confusion dominated her. He had been acting weird all day, but the ginger chicken he cooked was fantastic.

He ran his hand through his thick blond hair. "I'm making a mess of this. I've been trying to find out how long you're staying without coming right out and asking. So"—he drew in a deep breath—"how long will you be staying? And I don't mean in my living room." He made a quick look about and took her hands in his. "I mean here at Starvation Lake in the Davenports' cottage. How much longer do I get to have the pleasure of your company?"

Her heart raced miles ahead of her. "Well, I made indefinite plans with Josie's parents to use their place, and I have started paying them rent, though they protested. They have been so kind. I don't want to take advantage of them. Josie and her parents have other plans for Thanksgiving, but they intend to come up Christmas Day. So I suppose I will be staying at least through the Christmas holiday. After that I haven't a clue. Does that sufficiently answer your question?"

A broad grin dominated his face. "Well, about Thanksgiving, I insist you come over here. And I will not take no for an answer. Okay?"

"You just said I couldn't say no." Not that she wanted to.

"Good," he said with a nod. "I'm glad you're paying attention."

She had listened, but was there more to what he was saying than what was in his words? He made no effort to take her home before eight o'clock, but precisely at eight he drove her back to her cottage.

He took her in his arms and gave her a lingering good-night kiss. He pulled back from her but still held her securely in his arms. "I do believe you are addictive, Miss Lorelei Hayes." His voice was husky.

She gazed up at him. "Is that good or bad?"

"Very, very good." He leaned down for another quick kiss before making a hasty departure.

She watched him go. *You, too, Mr. Kessel, are very addicting. And I guess I'll have to quit cold turkey when it comes time to leave.*

twelve

The following Saturday Garth came by to spend the day with Lori, not that he hadn't spent every evening the past week with her. "You want to play a game?" Garth stood in front of her hearth with the giant bowl of popcorn they had just made.

"Okaaay. There are some in the little room." Lori headed in that direction. The request seemed a bit odd since he had never suggested a game before.

"I had something different in mind."

Her feet stopped in midstride, and she swung around to face him.

Garth's eyes were bright with delight. "Let's play 'I've got a secret.'"

Secret?

Her throat tightened, and her heart dropped to the pit of her stomach. Did he know? Of course not, how could he? But maybe he could sense she was holding something back, and this was his way to get her to come clean.

"It's easy. We take turns telling each other something about ourselves the other person doesn't know."

No, she wanted to shout. *Let's play something else—Boggle, Monopoly, Go Fish, anything.*

"Come on. It'll be fun. We'll learn interesting things about each other."

Fun?

"Please."

How could she get out of it without drawing attention to the fact that this honesty game scared her to death? "All right." How deep was this game supposed to be?

His smile broadened, and he took her hand, leading her over

111

by the fire. Lori never had fires; they scared her. But it was a cold night; it had been cold all day with the first snowflakes of the year falling, and Garth said he would tend to the fire. They sat down on the floor with the popcorn. Lori cradled the bowl on her lap for security or strength or something to hide behind, at least something to hide her shaking hands.

"You go first," he said.

"Me?" She cleared her throat. "This is your game—you go first."

"All right. Let's see." He put his finger to his chin as if to think. "My favorite color is green." He looked right into her eyes and smiled.

Lori had expected some sort of deep confession or secret. The knot in her stomach loosened.

"Your turn." He took a handful of popcorn and tossed some into his mouth.

"My favorite color is—"

Garth held up his hand to stop her. "Not fair. I can guess that one. Pick something I don't know."

"So what is it?"

"Purple."

"Wrong. Yellow."

"Really?" Disbelief replaced his smug grin.

"Your turn." Maybe this game would be fun after all.

"Then why do you have a purple car if it's not your favorite color?"

"Not fair. You didn't say anything about asking questions. I already told you something about me."

He grimaced at her then finally said, "I changed my major three times in college."

The expectant look on his face told her he was still waiting for the answer to his earlier question about her purple car.

"When I was little we had a dog named Butch. Your turn."

His jaw dropped, as if he didn't believe she hadn't answered his question yet. He recovered quickly and told her a trite bit of information.

"My brother chose the car for me," she said.

"Why would your—?" He stopped when she raised her eyebrows. He gritted his teeth. "This is supposed to be fun."

"I'm having fun." She smiled. "Your turn."

"I don't like being toyed with. Your turn."

"I don't like being pressured into talking about things. Your turn."

He paused. "I'm sorry. I let my curiosity get the better of me."

She nodded once. "Forgiven."

"Thank you," he said then continued the game. "We had a dog, too—a golden retriever named Pumpkin."

"Pumpkin?"

"Don't ask."

He was getting her back, making her curious. It wasn't that she didn't want to tell him; she didn't want to be forced into it. If she allowed this question, then he would feel free to ask others. It was a bad precedent. "My brother chose purple because it was better than pink."

He opened his mouth but closed it again, giving her a playful glare. "It was the fall, and the puppy lay down under a bush. All curled up she looked like a pumpkin."

"I couldn't drive, and my brother was tired of ferrying me around. I told him there was no point in learning to drive when there was no car for me to drive." She paused, caught off guard by his intense look of interest as he listened. "Knowing my justifiable fear of cars, he chose one with a reputation for safety and asked what color I wanted. I didn't want to have a car at all or even to drive. I preferred to depend on him. He knew it wasn't good for me, and I knew he wouldn't drop the car thing, so I told him I wanted purple. I told him pink would do just as well, knowing my brother would never subject any automobile to either one of those colors."

"But he called your bluff."

"He refused to drive it, calling it a giant grape on wheels. I think it looks more like a plum." She paused with a shiver of vivid recollection, another round of painful memories, and took a deep breath. "I miss him."

Garth squeezed her hand. "My turn." He paused and looked away. When he looked back at her, mischief danced in his eyes. "Do you remember that one summer you spent up here with Josie?"

"Vividly. It was the best summer of my life."

"It was the end of the summer, late in August. You went for a swim by yourself and rested out on the floating dock."

She struggled not to smile at the memory he was replaying. She remembered. How could she forget? The intensity of his eyes had always mesmerized her, not just their blue depths, but their look that was fathoms deep.

"It wasn't the lake's famous kissing bandit who kissed you. I was the boy who snuck up on the dock."

Though he had been serious, the smile she was trying to contain broke across her face. "I know."

His eyes widened. "How? I'm not that scrawny boy anymore."

"One thing that will never change is your eyes. At times I can still see you as that boy when you look at me. It's almost as if you are contemplating, trying to figure out some great mystery." Her voice dropped to a notch above a whisper. "Like now. They can be very hypnotic." She smiled.

A slow smile spread across his face. "I spent the whole two weeks we were up here trying to gather my nerve to talk to the pretty redheaded girl."

Lori felt her cheeks grow warm at his compliment.

"I felt a little like Charlie Brown." He ducked his head shyly but went on. "We, like most of the summer folks, would be returning to the real world. It was then or never. I was afraid you would disappear like a mermaid in the ocean never to be seen again. You were always with Josie. Your little swim seemed like my last and only chance to meet you alone. So I took a dive. Literally." He lifted his head. "I was only going to talk to you, but my mind went blank when I got up close to you. I didn't know what to say. I figured the bandit didn't have a half-bad idea." He took a handful of popcorn. "I looked for you all the next summer, but you never came back."

I would have if. . . She let the thought drift away like the bad dream it was.

"I guess it's your turn then," he said.

"That one didn't count. I already knew it was you," she said again.

"All right. Here's one you don't know."

She waited, uncomfortable with the silence, but he said nothing more. "Is it that bad? What did you do, put a snake in your sister's bed?"

He chuckled. "That was funny. You should have heard her scream. The humor died quickly, though, when my mom came in. That's when I knew I was in serious trouble."

"You didn't really?"

He nodded. "Afraid so. But it wasn't my fault. I was only seven, and my brother paid me to do it. I should have asked for double with the licking I got."

"Boys." She shook her head. "So what is this secret you are reluctant to tell me? It can't be as bad as the snake—"

He pierced her with his gaze, and all logical thought floated away. He reached out and touched her cheek. She had a feeling this was heading somewhere she did not want to go.

"I love you."

Caught off guard, she jumped to her feet, forgetting about the bowl of popcorn on her lap. Popcorn scattered everywhere.

"What?" It was more an accusation than a question.

He stood, too, the popcorn crunching under his feet as he stepped toward her. "That wasn't the reaction I was hoping for." He rubbed the back of his neck.

"This isn't happening." She stared up at him, grief stricken. "You can't be in—I mean, you're not supposed to fall—"

He put his hands gently on her upper arms. "I don't know if I'm supposed to or not. All I know is I *am* in love with you. If I'm not mistaken, your feelings are headed in that direction, too."

Heading in that direction? Her feelings had long since been there, camped out, and put down roots. "But—but—"

"What is so wrong with our falling in love with each other?"

"This isn't real. You're in love with an image you created from a fifteen-year-old girl you saw from afar. You fell in love with an ideal based on a ten-year-old memory."

"I'll agree that's partially true. But when we met, one of two things could have happened. One, I meet you, you are not all I imagined you to be, and the feelings fade away. Or, two, you are all I dreamed and more. You have a heart for the Lord. You are fun to be with, sensitive, kind, and gentle, and your beauty is more than skin deep; it goes clear through your soul. My feelings for you couldn't help but soar."

She looked away from him. He turned her face back to him with his finger under her chin. "Tell me you don't love me, too. Tell me you don't care in the least for me. Tell me you want me to leave and never come back, and I will."

She knew with one word from her he would go. She didn't want him to leave, ever. That was the problem.

"You can't, can you?" he said.

"No." Her voice was barely a whisper.

"Why do you do this? When we move forward to the next step in our relationship, you pull back."

"I'm afraid," she said softly.

"I'm afraid, too. Afraid of loving you so much you'll disappear like a dream upon waking. Afraid of not loving you at all and never knowing this feeling again. But my love for you keeps me pressing forward."

After a moment he lowered his lips to hers. He didn't pull her close, giving her the option of pulling away again. She leaned into him and extended her arms around his waist. Still he did not hold her but gently put his hands on her shoulders.

The surge of love she felt for him threatened to bubble over. She pulled back but left her arms around his waist. "I do love you."

He kissed her again. This time his arms held her securely in his love.

Why do I keep doing this? Dragging it out between us when I know it has to end. Each day only makes it worse, harder. I should have left weeks ago, months. I never should have come at all. The hurt she would inevitably cause him loomed closer each day. Drawn to him by some unseen force, she felt helpless to stop it. Her head said to leave before he did, but her heart held tightly to his. This was too good to last.

❧

The next week and a half flew by, and then Thanksgiving arrived. Lori wished she'd never agreed to spend the day at Garth's place. Had she known his parents were going to be there, she never would have consented. Never. "I'm nervous."

"Don't worry. My folks are great. They're going to love you almost as much as I do." He took her out to his SUV.

Hope and fear swirled recklessly inside her.

"My mom will love you instantly. In fact, she already does."

"How? She's never met me."

"She's heard about you." His crooked smile sent her heart fluttering with the butterflies in her stomach.

"And just where did she hear all about me?"

He shrugged. "My dad, on the other hand," he said thoughtfully, "will be the tough nut to crack. It'll take a good twenty seconds to win him over. Thirty tops."

"I see Gretchen's car and one for your parents, but who does the van belong to?"

"My oldest sister, Robin, and her family."

"What? You didn't tell me half your family was going to be here!"

"This isn't half my family, believe me. You knew my folks would be here."

"Not until last weekend."

"And you already know Gretchen. Robin's a bit more low-keyed than Gretchen. If you've met one sister, you've met them all."

She doubted his sisters thought they were all varying degrees of Gretchen. The deep breath she took did little to steady her erratic pulse.

Garth stepped out of his vehicle and walked around it. He scooped her up in his arms to carry her across the snow.

"Garth. Put me down."

He ignored her request and carted her up the porch, depositing her at the front door. The butterflies were out in full force in her stomach. At least Gretchen was there and obviously liked her. She would have one ally.

Garth's mother met them at the door with his father right behind her.

"This is my mom, Jolene, and my dad, George. Mom, Dad, this is Lorelei." Garth's general features were much like his dad's, but he had his mom's smile. Garth was a nice blend of both his parents.

After they had shaken hands and exchanged hellos, his father asked, "What's a cute little thing like you doing with this guy?" He pointed to Garth.

"George, behave yourself," his wife said.

"From all you have told us, Garth, I think she might be too good for you."

Great. What exactly has Garth told them?

"Unless—there's something wrong with her," he said in a hushed voice.

You want a list?

"There's absolutely nothing wrong with her. She's perfect." Garth hugged her from behind.

"Of course she is. George, and all of you, behave or you're going to scare her away before she even gets her coat off." His mom was stern but kind.

"We're only teasing," his dad said.

"See—I told you," Garth said softly over Lori's shoulder as he helped her with her coat. "Dad only teases people he likes."

His father turned back to Lori. "Don't mind my wife; she's not always so grumpy."

"Grumpy? If you don't shape up, I'll show you grumpy," his mom retorted.

"No, Jeannie was Grumpy," Gretchen said seriously, jumping into the conversation.

Everyone turned to her and burst out laughing except Lori. She didn't get the joke, and the knot in her stomach cinched a little tighter.

"Don't worry. You'll get used to them. They're harmless," said a brown-haired man several inches shorter than Garth. "Gretchen and Audrey dubbed each of the kids one of the seven dwarfs. Robin was Sleepy." He pointed to a female version of Garth's dad. "She was pregnant with Eamon at the time." He pointed to a teenage boy who was almost a duplicate of the man talking to her. "I think Garth, Ryan, and Gretchen were the only ones to retain their nicknames."

It made sense now. Garth often called Gretchen Happy, and she called him Bash, short for Bashful. She didn't see Garth as bashful, though maybe a bit reserved.

"I'm Mike, Robin's other half," said the man who had been explaining this family. "And this beauty is our daughter Carie, short for Caroline." He put his arm around an eleven-year-old girl who was a near image of her grandmother with long blond hair. "She's growing up too fast."

"Dad." She rolled her eyes.

Within no time she felt at home with Garth's family. Though they joked a lot, they shared a strong bond of love and loyalty. They had refused to let Lori bring any food and now shooed her out of the kitchen. She was *company*. She felt useless, though. But she liked this family. She liked it a lot. The family she didn't have.

After everything was cleaned up, Robin cornered Garth in the kitchen while he was sneaking another piece of pumpkin pie. Lori watched their serious conversation. Garth looked her way and smiled. Were they talking about her? She hoped not. Was his big sister telling him what she thought about his new girlfriend? Her throat tightened.

"Don't worry. My mom really likes you." Lori turned to Carie, whom she had been ignoring while her thoughts were caught up with the duo in the kitchen. "And I like you, too."

Lori smiled at this young jewel who so gently put her fears at ease. "Thank you."

"Grandpa likes you a lot, too. Grandma thinks he's going to scare you away." Her expression turned serious. "You won't be scared away, will you? You aren't really afraid of Grandpa?"

"No, I'm not afraid of your grandpa. And I won't be scared away." *At least not by him.*

"Good." The worry melted from her young face as she sighed. "Are you going skiing with us tomorrow?"

"No, I don't ski."

"I'll teach you." This girl had certainly taken a shine to her.

"I can't ski," Lori said.

"I'll stay on the bunny slope with you all day—I promise."

"I'm sure that wouldn't be any fun for you."

"I'll have fun. I promise. Please."

"Carie, if she doesn't want to go, don't pester her," Robin said. She and Garth had come over to where Lori and Carie were sitting on one of the couches.

"Yes, Mom. I'm sorry, Miss Hayes." The girl looked disappointed.

"It's not that I don't want to go; I really can't," Lori said. Yet another thing taken in the accident.

"Lorelei has a bad hip," Garth said. "It hurts her in the cold."

She glanced around at each member of Garth's family. The realization of the situation dawned on her. Garth loved her, and now she was spending a holiday with his family. She was here on approval! But he had invited her weeks ago, before he told her he loved her. He must have loved her long before he said so. She had loved him before that.

This wasn't good. She had to quit fooling herself that they were just friends. Just friends didn't spend every moment they could with each other. Just friends didn't kiss the way they did. And just friends didn't profess their love while gazing into each other's eyes.

She had let this go way too far. But how did she stop this train she had put into motion?

thirteen

On Tuesday the weather had turned decidedly wet. Garth stopped by Lorelei's directly from school as was his usual pattern. There was no point in going home for one second only to leave again. He stood at the kitchen sink filling the teakettle to make them both some cocoa on this cold, dreary day. Through the window he saw a man in a blue baseball cap walking down the driveway. He held his coat collar up around his neck, but it did little good against the torrential rain.

"Are you expecting company?" he asked Lorelei.

"No. You're the only one who knows where I live, and you're already here."

"Well, company's coming, dripping wet, down your driveway. Do you know him?"

Lorelei came up beside him as the man approached the cottage. "No. Must be someone for the Davenports."

Garth was glad he was there so Lorelei wouldn't have to greet a strange man alone. He set the kettle on the stove then pulled open the door before the man had a chance to knock. "Come in out of that awful weather." He knew the man had to be cold. If the temperature dropped a degree or two, this would be snow.

The man hesitated then entered only far enough to close the door behind him.

"May I take your coat?" Garth offered.

"No, thank you." The man removed his hat. "I won't be staying long."

Garth wasn't sure what to make of him. He seemed nervous, the way he toyed with his hat and darted glances at Lorelei but wouldn't look directly at her. The hair on the back of Garth's neck stiffened.

"Would you like to sit down?" Lorelei offered him a chair.

"No, thanks."

"The Davenports aren't here, but I would be glad to let them know you stopped by."

"I didn't come to see them."

Garth's uneasiness increased each moment this man remained. He avoided eye contact with Lorelei when he spoke to her.

The man swallowed hard. "I'm looking for Lorelei Hayes."

Garth's insides tightened.

"I'm Lori Hayes."

For the first time the man looked at her.

What did he want? "I'm Garth Kessel." Garth stuck his hand out for the man to shake. "And you are—?"

Though he shook Garth's hand, he didn't offer his name. If he had come to cause trouble for Lorelei, he would have to go through Garth first.

"Ray," the man finally said to Garth then turned to Lorelei. "Raymond Kent."

He kept his gaze glued on Lorelei as if waiting for a reaction. Garth looked at her, as well. Her sweet, welcoming smile faded to something akin to terror. All color drained from her normally rosy face.

"I came to apologize," Ray said.

"No," Lorelei said in a barely audible tone and took a step backward.

"I never meant to hurt anybody."

"Go away." She stepped back again.

The man took a step forward, his arms out, pleading. "If I could go back and change things, I would."

"I don't want to hear this! Haven't you caused enough damage?" She turned, nearly tripping over the coffee table in her flight to the bedroom, and slammed the door.

She may not have known this man by sight, but she obviously knew him by name. What had he done to cause such a reaction? If looks could kill, Ray Kent would be charred.

Ray dropped his hands to his sides and hung his head.

What should he do now? Say something? Throw the guy out? Demand an explanation?

Ray turned slowly and dug in his pocket for his wallet. He pulled out a business card and handed it to Garth. "In case she changes her mind." He refused to make eye contact.

Garth stared at the card as Ray moved to the door. Before he had a chance to step outside, Garth grabbed him by the arm. "What did you do to her?"

Slowly he raised his eyes to meet Garth's. "I'm the drunk driver who killed her parents."

Garth's hand slipped from Ray's arm. The man trudged up the hill, not bothering to put on his hat or ward off the rain in any way.

So he was the man who had caused Lorelei so much pain and anguish. Shouldn't Garth be angry, enraged? Instead he pitied the now-broken man who needed forgiveness from one who wasn't ready to give it.

The teakettle screeched, and Garth jumped. He removed it from the burner and took a deep breath. Lorelei! He rushed to the bedroom and knocked on the door. "Lorelei? Are you okay? May I come in?"

He heard a muffled yes.

Was that, yes, she was okay? Or, yes, he could come in?

He opened the door slowly, and his heart wrenched. In the middle of the double bed, she sat with her knees held tightly to her chest like a wounded animal. He knew enough to approach with extreme caution. "He's gone."

She burst into tears and sprang toward him. The grip she had on his neck made it easier for him to carry her to the couch in the living room. He held her and rocked her for a long time before she relaxed in his arms. The woman he loved continued to draw in shuddered breaths, while something boiled just under the surface within him.

"He walked away," she finally managed to say.

Like a whooped dog with his tail between his legs. "Yes, he's gone."

"No. From the accident. He walked away with barely a scratch."

Of course! Isn't that the way it always goes? The drunk whose fault it is rarely gets hurt or killed.

"He only did eighteen months in prison and five years' probation, and his license was permanently revoked. It isn't fair."

She took a jagged breath. "His headlights came straight at us. My dad tried to swerve and get out of his way, but it was too late. He just kept coming at us. Then we rolled over and over down the gully. My mom and I screamed and screamed; then suddenly she just stopped. I was the only one left to scream, and I couldn't anymore. All I could think was my new white Christmas sweater was ruined and I was going to die—and *he* walked away."

Garth clenched and unclenched his fist. He wanted to hit something, preferably Ray Kent. He knew it was wrong, but it was how he felt. He should pity the poor man, but that man had hurt the woman he loved.

Father, help me. I am so angry, and this feeling is strong; help me not to sin. I feel as if I have no control over it. I don't want to give in to this. I wouldn't be of any good to Lorelei then. She needs me right now. Help her, Lord; comfort her. Let her know that You and I are here for her.

As he prayed, he went from tense and uptight to more relaxed and calm. He would leave Ray in God's hands; he had to take care of Lorelei.

He caressed her hair. "Do you still want some cocoa? I can reheat the water."

"Cocoa sounds great. I'll make it. I need something to do."

As Garth watched her limp across the room, his anger welled up again. *Lord, I need Your peace. Please help me deal with this.*

He knew he would have to face these feelings again, but he knew the Lord would help him.

Lorelei picked up Ray's card from the counter where Garth had flipped it. "What's this?"

"Nothing." He took the card from her.

"Burn it."

"I'll take care of it." He shoved it into his pocket. "I'm sorry he came and upset you."

"I don't want to talk about it anymore. I don't even want to think about it."

"Sometimes it helps to talk."

"Not this, not anymore. I've talked to so many counselors about the accident and my feelings over the last ten years. It never does any good. It never changes anything. Everything remains the same, and life goes on." She took a deep breath. "I want to forget he ever came."

Pretending it never happened won't make it go away. "How about an ice cream cone in Mancelona?"

She shook her head with a shrug and took out two mugs from the cupboard. "I don't want to go out in the rain."

He realized it would only make her hip hurt more, reminding her of a man they would both like to forget. "What do you say if I run over to my place and grab a couple of squirt guns and we can have a water fight—indoors?" He wiggled his eyebrows up and down.

"I'll pass." But she did smile.

He wrapped his arms around her waist. "How about if I hold you and kiss you until you haven't a thought left in your pretty little head except of me?"

The kettle whistled, and he let her go. "Or maybe we could just have our cocoa?"

"That doesn't sound like a very good trade." She held the kettle over the mugs.

"So you liked my kissing idea?"

She batted her lashes at him and said demurely, "Well, Mr. Kessel, I don't know. I may need a little tutoring."

He had to refrain from laughing and sobered his expression. "Miss Hayes, I don't normally tutor my students." He almost couldn't maintain his façade with her eyelash batting. "But in your case I could make an exception, if it will help."

She broke down and laughed first. He joined her, relieved to see her bounce back so quickly.

&

Friday after Garth left, Lori headed for bed early. She hadn't slept well since Raymond Kent had invaded her life again. And when she did drop off, the nightmare came unrelentingly. She was so tired she had to sleep tonight.

"Lord, please take all thought of that man away from me and keep the nightmare away. I just want sleep."

"Forgive him."

What? She couldn't do that. He didn't deserve to be pardoned. She would not free him from his chains, not as long as she still suffered.

"Forgive him."

No. It was too much to ask. If she was forced to endure this pain the rest of her life, then so should he.

"Your unforgiveness holds you captive."

He didn't deserve it.

"Set him free. Set yourself free."

Forgiveness may set Ray Kent free, but she would still be held hostage in the body he mangled—and to the memories.

"Why are you here?"

She had asked herself that same question.

"Forgive him."

Is that why the Lord had brought her here, so Ray Kent could find her? So she would be forced to face him and finally let go? Could she let go of a bitterness she had clung to so tightly all these years?

fourteen

The next morning Lori pressed the disconnect button on the phone then dialed information again. She picked another name on the map. Sooner or later she would find the right town. "I need Your help, Lord. This isn't working." He lived somewhere in this state. Another dead end. She slammed down the phone and scribbled off another dot on her map.

She saw Garth's shadow darken the breezeway and opened the door before he knocked. An anxious look was on his face. "I tried calling several times, but your line was busy."

"I've been on the phone."

Garth picked up her map. "What did this poor map ever do to you?"

She glanced at it. "I'm looking for someone."

"Who?"

Could she even say the man's name to him? She took a deep breath. "Raymond Kent."

Garth's brows pulled together. "Why do you want to find him?"

"I don't want to; I need to. I need to forgive him. I think that's why God brought me back to Michigan."

Garth put his arms around her waist but held her so he could still see her face. "I thought you came back because of me."

Maybe she had. She didn't know. But one thing was certain; she must forgive the man, whether she wanted to or not.

"Are you sure about this?" Garth asked.

"Positive. I just can't find him. I think maybe I should hire a private investigator."

"That won't be necessary." Garth pulled out his wallet and handed her Ray's slightly mangled business card, with one corner charred.

She stared at it. "I thought you burned it."

"I tried, but a little voice warned me not to. I guess this was why."

"Thank you." She threw her arms around his neck.

He held her close. "When are you going?"

"Today."

He let go of her. "Now?"

"The sooner I do this, the sooner I can sleep at night."

He cupped her face. "I'm going with you."

"I was hoping you would." She gave him a weak smile. "I don't think I could face him alone."

He held her close, and she clung to him.

"I love you so much. I'll do almost anything for you," he whispered in her ear.

Though his words comforted her, they also caused her insides to tighten.

જી

Garth turned onto April Court, where several cars were sitting in front of a tan house. He pulled up the street and parked two doors away.

"Are you ready for this?"

Lori took a deep breath. "As ready as I'll ever be."

They walked back down the street. Lori stopped at the end of the cement walkway and stared up at the house. *He* was inside, and she must forgive him.

Oh, Lord, give me strength.

"Are your feet stuck to the pavement?" Garth said.

"I think so."

"The worst has already happened. All you have to do is say, 'I forgive you.' You don't even have to go inside."

"I know. I've told myself the same thing a hundred times."

Garth pressed gently on the small of her back to prod her forward. They could hear voices inside before they mounted the porch.

"Do you want to ring, or shall I?" he asked.

She reached out and pressed the button. Her heart dropped

to the pit of her stomach.

A brunette woman opened the door. "Hello. May I help you?"

Lori's mouth went dry. His wife? She couldn't speak. *Say something, anything. Hello would be good.*

"We're here to see Ray Kent," Garth said on her behalf.

Bless his heart.

"Ray's not here at the moment. Would you like to come in and wait for him?"

"No, thank you," Lori managed to squeeze out of her tightening throat.

"Let me get his wife for you," the woman said and left.

"How are you doing?" Garth asked.

"Okay." Now she knew how Ray had felt when he came to her, nervous and reluctant to step inside.

A moment later a woman with long blond hair stood at the door with an infant on her shoulder. "Come in, please. I don't want the baby to get chilled."

Reluctantly Lori stepped inside, and Garth closed the door behind them.

"I'm Kim, Ray's wife. Ray ran to the store. Is there anything I can do for you?" The house was crowded with people.

"This looks like a bad time. We can come back later," Lori said.

"May I tell Ray what this was about?"

"Auntie Tim." A little boy pulled on her sleeve. "Tan I have a tookie?"

"Go ask Aunt Dotty."

"We'll come back later." Lori could almost feel the walls closing in on her. She turned and moved around Garth to get to the door. To escape.

"Are you Lorelei Hayes?" Kim asked in a rush.

Lori's hand froze on the knob. She couldn't move. She couldn't talk. All she could do was stare at the white door with dirty little handprints on it.

"Yes, she is," Garth said.

"Please don't go," Kim said softly and placed her hand gently on Lori's shoulder. "Ray will be very disappointed if he finds out he missed you. He has been praying for this opportunity for years. Please."

Lori released the knob and faced the woman.

"Thank you," Kim said to Lori then turned and spoke to the room of people. "Can you all take your party downstairs, please? I need the living room."

As they left the room, the other people nodded a greeting to them.

"Please have a seat. Would you like something to drink?"

Lori shook her head.

"I'll have some water," Garth said as they sat on the worn beige love seat. The kitchen chatter moved to the basement, as well.

Kim returned with the water. "Are you sure I can't get you anything?"

Lori shook her head again. She wasn't sure she could hold on to a glass right now.

Kim sat on the sofa opposite them. "You don't know how much this will mean to Ray. He should be back any minute."

They sat in awkward silence.

"What's your baby's name?" Garth asked.

"Rachel." Kim moved the sleeping child from her shoulder so they could see her.

"That's a beautiful name," he said.

"She's cute." Lori stared at the baby, who was squishing up her face at having been disturbed. *Adorable.* Ray Kent had a baby. . .a home. . .a family. He had everything that had been taken from her.

"Would you like to hold her?" Kim offered Lori.

"No, thank you."

Garth took her lead and declined, as well.

The room was blanketed in silence once again, except for the low din of voices and laughter coming up the stairs.

"Ray doesn't drive; they took his license away because of

the accident; he could petition the courts and probably get it back, but he says it's a small price to pay considering all you had to go through." She finally took a breath. She was as nervous as Lori and grasping at anything to say. Lori felt sorry for her. "My brother drove him to the store." Kim paused.

"But good things can come out of bad. Ray became a Christian through the prison ministry. He hasn't had a drop to drink since and won't even allow it in the house."

Lori didn't want to hear his life story; she just wanted to get this over with and leave. The man who took everything from her had everything. She stared at the baby. Once more, silence stretched out between them.

"I don't know what could be keeping them. They should have been back by now." She seemed to need to fill the silence. "That day we went up to your place, he was so disappointed; but he understood. Really he did."

Finally the back door opened and closed. "There he is now." Kim jumped to her feet and headed out of the room.

"Ray, you have visitors in the living room," Lori heard another woman in the kitchen say.

"I had a whole house full of visitors when I left. What did you do with them all?"

"Ray, Lorelei Hayes is here," she heard his wife say then. There was silence in the kitchen then feet scuffling down the stairs.

Lori's mouth went dry. She grabbed Garth's water and took several swallows, but it did no good.

Ray and Kim came in and sat on the sofa together. Kim held her husband's hand in support as Garth was holding Lori's. No one spoke for a moment. They all seemed to know this was the moment of truth. And it was all up to Lori. They were waiting for her to impart forgiveness.

I can't do this. I can't do this. I can't do this!

"Yes, you can," a soft inner voice said.

I don't want to do this.

"*Ah! There's the truth. It always comes down to your will or Mine.*"

Then Ray said, "I know it's a small thing to say I'm sorry, but I am truly, truly sorry for all the pain I caused you and your family."

I don't have any family, thanks to you!

"*Be strong and know that I am with you,*" the inner voice assured her.

"I feel some sense of relief being able to say that to you," Ray said. "And I know it's a lot to ask, but"—he took a deep breath—"would you forgive me?"

She recalled a verse from Isaiah: "*Do not fear, for I am with you; do not be dismayed, for I am your God. I will strengthen you and help you; I will uphold you with my righteous right hand.*"

A peace washed through her, taking her anger and bitterness away. "I forgive you." She was surprised she actually meant it. She felt a heavy burden lift from her. Garth squeezed her hand.

"Thank you. I know how hard that was for you, and I don't deserve it."

"No one does, but our heavenly Father forgives us freely with a lot less trouble."

They spoke for a few more minutes; then Lori and Garth left.

"You did well, sweetheart." Garth stopped beside his SUV. "I'm proud of you."

"I didn't realize how heavy the burden of unforgiveness was until I let it go," she said. "Thank you for coming with me and for saving that card."

"I'm glad to help in any way I can. Are you ready to head back up north?"

"Not just yet. Would you mind taking me to the cemetery where my parents are buried?"

Garth drove to the cemetery and parked. "Do you want me to come with you?"

"No. This is something I have to do alone." She walked across the snow-covered ground to her parents' graves, leaving fresh tracks in the inch of fresh powder.

"I did it. I forgave him. Not only for what he did to me but for you, too. I feel as if I can say good-bye to you now. Even though I have no one, I know it is going to be all right. Well, I do have Garth—for now anyway. I love him, but he doesn't know all about me yet. I'm afraid to tell him, afraid he will leave. Right now I feel vulnerable and need someone to cling to." Finally her life could go on.

She heard the snow crunch a short distance away and turned to see Garth standing nearby. When she looked at him, he came the rest of the way to her. "I didn't mean to intrude. I wanted to be here to help you if your hip hurt from being out in the cold."

She smiled up at him. He was always so thoughtful. His care and concern warmed her, but sadness clutched her heart.

He gazed at the side-by-side graves. "I wish I could have met them."

Lori echoed his sentiment, not just because it would mean everything would be different, but because she knew her parents would have loved Garth almost as much as she did. "I'm finished here."

"Do you want me to carry you?"

"No, I think I can walk." He patiently remained at her side as she hobbled along painfully, his arm firmly around her waist for support. "I guess I was wrong." Before she finished her sentence, he swooped her up in his strong, loving arms.

fifteen

Two nights later Lori grasped her cup of cocoa as she listened to the wind howling through the trees. Up and down. In and out. It woke her, and rather than lie awake listening she got up to do something, anything.

She knew the roar of a hurricane, but this moaning that sounded like a mother mourning for her lost children crept inside her. She had to take her mind off the agonizing groaning, so she chose an upbeat tune from one of the CDs. Softly at first then louder to drown out the wailing. She slumped down on the couch.

The wind punished the rain, lashing it against the windows, turning it into ice and sleet, and whipping it across the roof. The lights flickered. She held her breath for a moment, glad they didn't go out.

The music soothed her, though she could still hear the storm in the background. She sipped her cocoa and relaxed a little. Deep even breaths. Another flicker, then suddenly she found herself in terrifying silent blackness except for the freezing rain and ice pelting the windows. Her cup hovered halfway between her lap and her mouth, and her blood ran cold. Her hands began to tremble, spilling cocoa on her lap.

Garth! She would call Garth. It was pretty much a straight shot across the cottage to the phone if she remembered to step around the coffee table.

Darkness had enveloped her the night of the accident, and darkness came as smoke the night of the fire, suffocating her. She couldn't breathe; it was so hard to breathe.

Her hands shook more violently now, but she managed to feel the buttons and dial Garth's number. She hoped Garth wouldn't mind being awakened in the middle of the night if he knew she had no electricity.

The phone wasn't ringing. She hung up to dial again but couldn't get a dial tone.

NO!

The phone couldn't be out, too.

Behind the curtains, pellets of sleet drummed against the rattling windows. She realized her isolation. No one else could help her. The storm worsened with each passing minute. *Lord, help me.*

All she needed was a little light, and she would be fine. She rummaged through a nearby drawer then remembered seeing a flashlight in the cupboard, a silver one. She knocked out a small basket with pens, pencils, and a pair of scissors. She heard them scatter as they hit the floor.

The flashlight also careened to the floor, bouncing off the counter. She fumbled for it but couldn't see what she was groping for. She knelt down among the array of pens and pencils and spread them further in her search for the light. She laid her hands on the flashlight and pushed the switch up.

Nothing. She shook it and hit it and rapped it on the floor. Still no saving light. Her breathing became short and rapid.

The mantel. A candle. Matches.

On her hands and knees she crawled to the fireplace and found the long wooden matches. She stood up on the hearth and located a candle. Her breathing still came in short gasps. Her head began to spin from lack of oxygen. She tried to draw in a long, slow breath, but her lungs refused to expand.

The candle. She had to concentrate on the candle. The lid of the matches tumbled to the floor. One long match slid out, and she set the canister on the mantel; but it, too, toppled to the floor.

Grasping the candle in her shaking hand, she readied the match then hesitated. The thought of purposely lighting a fire still terrified her, but could she handle being in utter darkness much longer? It would only be one small flame. It would be okay.

She located the mortar between two of the bricks and

struck the match. A spark but no flame. She did it again, harder and faster this time. And again. And again!

She stumbled off the hearth and searched for the rest of the matches. They weren't there, anywhere. Her lungs tightened, and air seemed even more scarce. *Cough. Cough.* Then the light came, far off in the distance, a dim glow. Closer and closer. It was coming to get her. She struggled to get a breath; the smoke was too thick.

❧

Garth banged on the door louder. Rain and ice fell from his coat as he did. "Lorelei!"

He turned and hunted for the key behind the hanging shelf in the small breezeway. Right where Mr. Davenport said it would be.

Immediately he saw the pens scattered across the kitchen floor and the phone receiver dangling. His heartbeat quickened. "Lorelei?"

He scanned the small interior for her with his light. Kneeling in front of the fireplace, she held a candle in one hand and a matchstick in the other. She shied away and raised her arms in front of her face to block the light. He diverted the beam and came to her.

She slapped at him and pushed him away. "No! No!"

He cupped her head in his hands and turned her to face him. "Lorelei, it's me, Garth."

Her eyes finally focused. "Garth?" She clutched him around the neck. "It was so dark. I couldn't see anything."

"It's all right. I'm here now." He caressed her hair and held her close.

She relaxed in his embrace, and her breathing became slow and even. "Thank the Lord you're here."

"I want to be here." *Always.* He took a deep breath. "Are you all right? You didn't hurt yourself stumbling in the dark?"

"I'm fine. I just couldn't get any light."

"As long as you are sure you're okay, I'll go ahead and start a fire."

"No!" She sat up straight. "I don't want a fire."

"I know fires scare you, but I promise it will be safe. With no electricity the furnace won't run, and this place will get cold real fast."

She nodded her consent. Within minutes a fire blazed. He turned to her and said, "You have any marshmallows?"

"I thought you were the Boy Scout. Didn't you come prepared?" Her words were strained, and she tried to smile but couldn't.

He snapped his fingers. "I knew I forgot something." He pointed at her then. "I made you smile."

"Thank you, Garth, for everything. I feel really silly for panicking and losing it there for a minute."

"Now you *are* being silly." He sat on the couch next to her. "Total darkness can play funny tricks on the mind. People have gone crazy without light."

"Are you calling me crazy?" she said playfully.

"Never. But I am. Crazy about you." He leaned over and kissed her. "Why don't you lie down here on the couch and try to get some sleep? I'll keep watch over the fire."

"I'm not tired."

The circles under her eyes told him otherwise. "Humor me."

She lay down, but she refused to close her eyes. He pulled the blue and white afghan from the back of the couch over her.

"You can't sleep if you don't close your pretty green eyes."

Her worried gaze darted to the fire and back at him.

He gazed at her for a few moments then said, "Do you mind if I ask you a question?"

"What?"

"I've noticed that Josie and everyone else calls you Lori and you introduce yourself as Lori, but you asked me to call you Lorelei. Why is that?"

"Actually you asked me if you could call me Lorelei. I merely said yes. If I failed to mention that no one calls me that, my oversight."

"Do you prefer Lori? I can start calling you that, as well."

"I kind of like your calling me something different from everyone else. It makes it. . .special."

He looked at her and smiled. "How about 'my love'? That's special. Or sweetheart or honey or darling?"

Lori smiled. "Those are good, too."

He tucked the afghan around her. He settled himself in front of the couch, leaning against it, and took one of her hands in his. He kissed the back of it gently. This was where he was supposed to be. He leaned his head back, thanking the Lord for the wonderful turn in his life this fall.

❧

Lori wiggled her foot under the claw-footed table. Eyeing the empty chair across from her, she had an odd sensation something was up. Garth had never taken her to this restaurant before. This was first class. They usually ate at fast-food places or family-style restaurants before or after church. Once they ate at a Mexican restaurant, but that was still casual—nothing ever this expensive.

His manner and behavior were unnerving, as well. He had taken extra care with his attire, she could tell. His best suit. She had only seen him wear it to church once. He looked nice—stunning, in fact.

When Garth returned to the table, he gave her his most captivating smile. A lump formed in her throat, and her pulse raced. Something *was* up. She forced a smile. She hated surprises.

She wanted to run. She wanted to hide. She wanted the wing chair she was sitting in to swallow her.

Their waiter, in a black satin vest and bow tie, returned with the dessert menus.

"No, thank you. I'm stuffed." Would that hasten her escape from this softly lighted trap? She could pretend to feel ill, which wouldn't be stretching the truth. What was he up to?

"Order something," Garth said. "I'm getting the cheesecake."

"Really, I'm full."

He lowered his menu, and his gaze locked with hers. "Please."

Why resist? She couldn't say no to him. Not that she wanted to. Her resolve slipped away as she looked at his impish smile.

"She'll have the strawberry cheesecake, also."

"I don't like cheesecake." She offered no alternative selection.

He studied her through squinty eyes and took up the challenge. "Chocolate mousse?"

So it was guess-the-dessert now. "Too rich."

He studied her a moment longer; then his smile broadened in triumph. "The lady will have a dish of vanilla ice cream with strawberries." Though he spoke to the waiter, his gaze never left her. Laughing. Adoring. Intense. Loving. The uneasy feeling in the pit of her stomach crept up her spine.

With no objection from her, the waiter left and returned a minute later with their order. That was fast. He set Lori's ice cream in front of her and paused. She thanked him, and he immediately set Garth's cheesecake in front of him. He hesitated and eyed her again. She said thank-you again to the still-hovering waiter, who was staring at her. He mustn't have heard her the first time. Attentive was one thing; this waiter was bordering on obnoxious. He walked away and spoke to another waiter and waitress lingering nearby. Didn't they have work to do? Customers to wait on?

She looked to Garth, who also stared at her expectantly. Why was everyone so interested in her? Did she have food on her face or something?

She figured it must be the *or something* because of the adoring way Garth looked at her. He was devouring every inch of her face as he had done ten years ago with that look of contemplation in his eyes. Then he was debating whether to kiss her or not. What was on his mind tonight?

"Have some ice cream," he finally said and took a bite of his cheesecake.

"I really am full." She pushed the dish away.

Garth looked up at her and set his fork down. He glanced at her ice cream and back up at her. "Just one bite?"

One bite. She could do that. And he seemed to want her to, for some strange reason. He had never been so insistent about anything before.

She picked up the spoon and moved her dish closer. Garth watched her every move intently, almost nervously. What was so important about a little ice cream? She soon discovered, and her hand froze in midair. The spoon slipped from her grip, hit the dish and the saucer beneath it, then came to a noisy conclusion against her glass.

She clasped her hand over the spoon to stop the clattering, which was fruitless since it had already made all the noise it was going to. Staring at the dessert didn't change anything. The ice cream was covered with a generous amount of fresh-cut strawberries and a dollop of whipped cream with a cherry on top. Threaded over the stem of the cherry sat a solitaire diamond ring.

"Surprise."

That was an understatement. She looked up at Garth, whose eyes were wide and bright with expectation, then at the other diners nearby who were staring at them. The number of waiters and waitresses congregated now numbered six. Suddenly the small room seemed to close in on her. Heat rushed up her cheeks.

Why did he do this to her in a public place? So she couldn't turn him down? So she couldn't run and hide? Run is exactly what she felt like doing. Now the whole evening made sense, his attentiveness to her and every last detail of their intimate dinner for two at the most expensive restaurant in town.

He had made it impossible for her to say no, at least not here, not now.

Garth slid his chair back, rescued the ring from the cherry, and knelt down on one knee beside her. "I was going to give this to you for Christmas, but I can't wait that long." He held the ring in his hand. "Will you marry me?" His eyes were alight with hope.

Just like a fairy tale. She always imagined it like this. Or was she dreaming? Everyone she ever loved died. How could this be a fairy tale? "Garth. I—I don't know what to say."

"Yes would do my heart a world of good."

"But you hardly know me. There are things you don't know about me."

"I know you know the Lord. You're smart and witty and a lot of fun to be with. You're loving and caring and beautiful, and I love you more than anything on this earth. And I want to spend the rest of my life learning everything there is to know about you."

"But what if there is something you don't like and can't live with?"

"If that were the case, God would have made that clear. I have prayed a lot about this." He took her hand and held the ring over it. "Marry me." His eyes beckoned her to say yes.

"Can it work, Garth? Can it really work?"

"Yes." He held the ring to her finger. "It's as easy as this." He slid the ring on her finger. She didn't stop him.

The onlookers erupted in applause, and Garth embraced her.

Technically she hadn't said yes, but she did let him put the ring on her finger—against her better judgment. Maybe it could work out for them. Maybe they could have a future. She was beginning to believe anything was possible with him.

sixteen

Lori looked forward to spending Christmas Day with Garth's family. Holidays were meant for families. Since she no longer had a family she would borrow his, so loving and accepting of her. She thought it might work out between Garth and her. After Christmas, when his family had left, she would tell him everything. That way she wouldn't spoil the holiday. Then they could talk through things without an audience, or they wouldn't, and she could go away to suffer in peace. But she wouldn't think about that now. She was going to enjoy today.

Garth strode down the snowy hill, and her stomach clenched in a knot. His whole family was supposed to be there today. All six of his brothers and sisters with spouses and children. Now, as Garth's fiancée, she was to be presented to his entire clan. Was she ready for this?

Garth knocked, and she jumped, her heart racing. Lori wished they could stay here and not go over to his place and face the crowd that was already assembled and awaiting her arrival.

"Before we go"—he handed her a gift-wrapped box—"this is for you. Merry Christmas."

She held up her left hand, wiggling her ring back and forth. "I thought this was my Christmas present."

"Is there a law that says a man can't give the woman he loves more than one Christmas present?" He caressed her cheek with his hand.

It warmed her heart every time he said he loved her. Would she ever tire of it? "No, no law." She took a deep breath then tore her gaze from his and opened her package like an excited child. Inside lay a beautiful blue and green sweater, the one she'd put back at the woolen shop.

"When did you go back?" She held it against herself.

"I didn't."

She looked up at him curiously and smiled. "You bought it that day?"

"I couldn't let you be deprived. Besides, it brings out the color in your eyes." He held out his hand to her. "Ready to meet the rest of the family?"

"Just a minute." She trotted off to her room with the sweater in hand. She took off the white wool sweater she had on and replaced it with her new blue and green one.

Garth beamed with satisfaction. If only she could save that look in a bottle and have it for all time. "Now I'm ready."

He escorted her to his vehicle and drove her to his family's cottage. He came around to the passenger side and picked her up to carry her through the snow.

"Garth, I can walk."

He smiled. "Sneakers are not appropriate snowshoes. We should have gotten you some boots in Traverse City." He smiled and swung her up in his arms. "But I'm glad we didn't."

"Promise you'll put me down on the first step of the porch. I don't want your family to see you carrying me."

"Why?" He stopped several feet from the porch. "I carried you at Thanksgiving."

"Please, Garth. It's embarrassing. I don't want anyone to see."

"You mean anyone who isn't already peeking out the window at us?"

Lori turned and glimpsed several faces disappearing from the glass. "This is embarrassing." She wondered how red her face was.

Garth chuckled.

"I'll get you for this."

"Promises, promises." He moved the rest of the way to the porch and stopped to set her down. But the door jerked open.

"Practicing, little brother?" One of Garth's brothers stood in the doorway.

Lori could feel the blush deepening.

Garth continued up the steps with her.

She gritted her teeth. "Put me down."

"No point now." He smiled and winked. When he finally did set her down inside the cottage, more than a dozen pairs of eyes were looking at her.

"Isn't it a little soon to be practicing for carrying her over the threshold?" a male voice said from the group. She couldn't tell whom. She was afraid to look at any of them.

"Unless of course they eloped," the man from the doorway said.

"He wouldn't dare. Mom would kill him," a woman said.

"If you're smart, you will. I thought about it," the same man confessed.

"Blake, you didn't?" Garth's mom said.

"I couldn't stand all the fuss you made over Robin's and Jeannie's weddings. You can thank your daughter-in-law that we didn't." Blake turned back to Garth and said in a conspiratorial whisper, "Elope."

"I heard that," his mom said. "Garth, don't even entertain the idea."

Gretchen broke through the crowd. "Lori!" She flung out her arms and embraced her. "Company comes, and they act like a flock of squawking birds."

Ignoring the others, Gretchen took her away to meet the children, who seemed to be behaving better than the adults. She began naming them off, but Lori couldn't keep up.

"Gretchen, bring her back. We haven't even introduced anyone," someone called from the group, and Lori turned back to them.

"Garth, you should make the introductions," his mother said.

Lori searched out Garth's face; to look at everyone at once was overwhelming. Garth stepped away from them, smiling at her. "Family, this is my *fiancée* and love of my life." He came up beside her and wrapped a possessive arm around her, gazing down at her lovingly. "Lorelei, the most wonderful woman in the world."

Lori felt her face warm at Garth's introduction, but she had never felt more loved and cherished in her life. They *could* make it work.

"Garth, you're embarrassing her. Typical male. We know who she is. Mom wanted you to introduce all of us to her." A dark-blond woman stepped forward and extended her hand. "I'm Jeannie, one of Garth's older sisters."

Gretchen spoke then. "And this is the rest of the family. No point in introducing everyone at once; it would be too hard to remember. You'll have years to figure it out and who goes with whom."

Lori counted seventeen or eighteen people. She kept getting a different number. She understood now why Garth had such a large table, but even its grand size wouldn't accommodate everyone there. The children were served first at the table, and the adults scattered throughout the house with their plates. She liked this crazy family. Being part of it helped her not miss her own family as much.

After the chaos of eating and cleaning up was over, the adults sat around, well fed and droopy eyed. Garth was lying on the floor with eight-year-old Dustin beside him playing a video game on the TV.

"Hannah, get off Uncle Garth," Ruth said to her three-year-old daughter, who was bouncing on Garth's back.

"I don't mind. She can stay. If I want her off, all I have to do is"—he reached behind him and grabbed the girl, rolling over as he did—"tickle her."

Hannah squealed with delight. Dustin put aside his game controller and jumped on, joining the fun. Five-year-old Mary came over cautiously and joined in, too, warming up quickly to the antics.

A small amount of Lori's hope seeped out, watching Garth with his nieces and nephew.

Carie and Eamon scrambled upstairs then, abandoning

their Ping-Pong game. "Can we deck-jump, Uncle Garth?" Eamon asked.

"If it's okay with your folks."

"Mom said we had to ask you, since this is mostly your place."

"Then let's go." Garth stood up with the three children hanging from his arms and back.

"Can I go?" Dustin asked.

"Can I go?" Mary asked.

Dustin was given permission, but Ruth refused Mary's request.

"It's safe, Ruth. I promise." Garth placed one hand over his heart.

"Please, Mommy."

Lori wondered what deck-jumping was and was going to ask, but the scene was a little too chaotic.

"Ruth, let her go," Blake said on his daughter's behalf.

"Okay," she finally said. "But be careful."

Garth held up one hand. "I'll take personal responsibility."

"I want to go, too," Hannah said.

"Absolutely not!" Ruth would not budge on that one.

There was a rustle of coats and snow pants as half the household prepared to go out.

"Come on, Audrey." Gretchen threw a coat to her sister.

"I'm not going." Audrey threw the coat back. Audrey was a year or two older than Gretchen and a newlywed of six months.

"Why not?"

"Because I don't want to."

"Come on. It'll be fun, like when we were kids." Gretchen continued to pester her, and Lori could see that Audrey's patience with her little sister was wearing thin.

"Why not?"

"Because it wouldn't be safe for the baby," Zach blurted out in his wife's defense.

Audrey glanced at him then lowered her head. Zach put

his arm around her. "I'm sorry. I know you wanted to wait."

"Baby?"

"You're pregnant?" The questions flew from all sides.

"How far along are you?" Everyone gathered around the couple, congratulating them.

Lori ached inside.

"Eight weeks," Audrey said.

"Why didn't you tell us?"

"Because I knew you would all make a big fuss—like you're doing now." She was on the verge of tears. "This is supposed to be Garth and Lori's day. I didn't want to take the attention away from them." She turned to Garth. "I'm sorry."

"Don't be sorry. I think it's great." Garth gave her a hug and shook Zach's hand.

After the congratulations ceased, the struggle to get into snow gear continued.

"Would you hold Elizabeth while I help Mary?" Ruth said, placing the three-month-old in Lori's arms. Then she left to assist her oldest daughter.

Lori cuddled the baby and caressed her fuzzy head. Garth came over bundled up for the outside and said softly, "That looks good on you."

She didn't understand.

"A baby in your arms." Adoration sparkled in his loving eyes.

Oh, Garth. She wanted to cry.

He winked at her before following the others out the door, another bit of her hope going with him. Those left inside gathered around the windows to witness the event.

Lori stared in horror as Garth and the younger children climbed over or through the deck railing and held on. The older ones, including Ryan and Gretchen, stood on top of the rail.

Were these people crazy? They were a whole story up from the ground.

Someone counted to three, and they all jumped. Lori gasped

as they disappeared below. Hannah clapped her hands.

Garth's mom chuckled then touched her shoulder. "We should have warned you."

She saw soon enough that all were well. They had landed on a soft cushion of snow several feet below. Soon two snow forts were being constructed, and a snowball fight ensued.

She watched as Garth played with his nieces and nephews. How could she be so foolish? She was living in a fantasy world; she and Garth were isolated up here, just the two of them. That wasn't real life. Real life involved so many more people. She looked down at the sleeping baby in her arms, and the remainder of her hope died away.

She felt gratitude mixed with reluctance when Ruth took the child from Lori's arms. The women now wanted to talk wedding plans.

"Have you set a date yet? I assume it will be sometime this summer."

"No, we haven't." Lori's mouth went dry, her throat tight. She doubted there ever would be a date.

"I think this is our cue to go downstairs, boys." Blake headed for the stairs, the other men following after him.

"I know it seems like a long time, but summer will be here before you know it. We should start making plans right away."

Someone took out paper and pen. Lori found herself nodding in agreement to almost everything the committee came up with. She didn't care; her heart wasn't in it. Could any of it happen?

Gretchen and Mary came inside, and the conversation turned to babies. Lori didn't know which topic was worse—weddings or babies. She moved back to the window, watching Garth as she listened to the women chattering.

"Don't you think Garth and Lori will have the most beautiful children? I hope they all have her hair. Isn't it the most incredible color?" Gretchen prattled on.

The outside crew was now building a huge snowman on the frozen lake.

"Mom, I don't know how you did it seven times," Jeannie said.

"One at a time," her mother said. "I wouldn't do it any differently. But I am glad you girls are the ones having the babies now instead of me."

Hot tears stung Lori's eyes. She hurried to the bathroom and willed them away but knew they wouldn't be put off long. Retrieving her coat, she had it on and buttoned before anyone noticed.

"Are you going out to join the fun?" Garth's mom came up to her.

"I have a headache." It was true; her head did hurt. "I'm going to walk home."

"I thought maybe you weren't feeling well. All of us can be a bit much for someone who isn't used to a crowd. Here—let me get George to take you," she said.

"Please don't bother him. The fresh air will do me good. It's not that far." Lori hurried out the door, grateful she didn't try to detain her.

❧

Garth stomped off as much snow from himself as he could and began brushing off Dustin's back and front and legs. The kid was covered. "Remember to leave your wet shoes and gloves outside on the porch. You don't want Grandma getting after you for tracking snow all over the house."

They piled through the door with a roar and quickly shed their coats.

"Garth." His mother motioned him into the kitchen just inside the door.

"Let me get my boots off."

"That can wait." She led him into the kitchen, away from the flurry.

"This must be important to risk tracking snow inside." He glanced down at the snow melting from his boots. When he and his brothers and sisters were growing up, his mother had kept after them not to track the outdoors inside the cottage.

In winter it was snow; the rest of the year it was sand from the beach.

"Never mind about that. I wanted to let you know Lori left. She seemed a little upset and said she had a headache."

"When? Who took her?" She hadn't waited for him?

"About twenty minutes ago. She walked."

His stomach twisted. "She can't walk that far."

"Garth, I know you love her and want to protect her, but she is a grown woman."

"She has a bad hip." He touched his right hip. "The cold makes it hurt. She really can't walk that far, not in the freezing snow." Near panic, he donned his coat and raced to his truck. Whatever possessed her to walk in this cold?

જ

Lori held on to the mailbox, gathering up the strength to move on. If she were normal, she would have been home by now; as it was, she was only at the top of Garth's long driveway. Whatever made her think she could walk home in the cold? She should have had someone drive her, but she desperately needed to get away from them. All of them.

She wiped the tears from her face and forged her way to her next point. Making it the five steps to the garbage bin, she hoped the wood-framed, wire-mesh box would support her weight as she leaned heavily on it. It was designed to keep little critters out of the trash, not hold the weight of a grown woman. She scooted her way to the other end, each step more difficult than the last.

She heard a vehicle come up Garth's drive and slide to a stop on the road. No doubt a dark blue SUV. She knew who was driving even without looking. His door opened, and the snow crunched under his feet as he hurried over to her.

"Sweetheart, what are you doing?" He came up next to her and touched her arm.

She jerked away from him. She didn't want his endearment or his sympathy or him, for that matter, right now. She wanted to walk. To be normal. To be whole. "I'm walking home," she said through gritted teeth.

"If you want to go home, I'll take you." Concern etched his voice.

"I want to walk. I just want to be able to walk. Is that too much to ask?" She pushed away his helping hand as she let go of the garbage bin. "I can do it myself!" After two painful steps she dropped to her knees in the snow and cried.

"Please let me drive you," he pleaded.

She didn't resist when he picked her up and put her in his truck. She couldn't walk. She wasn't normal and never would be.

seventeen

Lori's knuckles were as white as the snow falling down outside her car for the grip she had on the steering wheel. If she could just make it to the highway and get off these slippery back roads, she would be fine.

She had to leave. It was best this way. If she stayed, Garth would try to change her mind. Leaving was the only way. Late into the night she realized sooner was better than later.

The flakes were getting bigger and falling more thickly. *Slap, slap, slap.* Back and forth went her wipers, but they did little good. She leaned forward over the steering wheel. Still she could barely see ten feet in front of the car.

She questioned her logic in leaving the safety of the little cottage. Heading back was her best option even if it meant facing Garth with a false smile and enthusiasm. She slowed at the bend in the road, looking for a driveway or street to turn around in.

The rear of the car fishtailed. She slammed on the brakes, and the car slid. No! Not again! *Please, God, help me.*

❧

Garth had a spring in his step as he approached the Davenports' cottage. It had been less than twenty-four hours since he had seen Lorelei, but the thought of seeing her caused his heart to beat so hard it threatened to leap from his chest. And he thought of her a lot. His family teased him mercilessly about his constant grin, but he didn't care. Love was grand.

She had looked so peaceful sleeping the day before and would be feeling better today.

Josie opened the door. He had left Lorelei with her the day before and felt better having someone there with her. But Josie's troubled expression did nothing to relieve him now.

"Hi, Garth."

"Hi. How's Lorelei?"

"She asked if you could deliver this for her." Josie handed him a small package wrapped in floral paper and tied with a pink ribbon, attached to a purple envelope. "She said she's really sorry to miss Carie's birthday party." Her face was pale.

An ominous sense of dread grew with each word. His smile wavered. Something was wrong. "Is it her hip?" he asked, tugging off his gloves. "Is it still hurting her?" He glanced in the direction of her room.

"That's not it."

"I'm going to check on her."

"Garth—"

Something *was* wrong. He tried to swallow the rising lump in his throat. If he could just see her— "I won't wake her. I promise." He headed toward her bedroom door.

"She's not there."

Garth paused. What did she mean, she wasn't there? He continued to the door and pulled it open. He stared at the neatly made bed with his two sweaters and sweatshirt stacked on it. All her stuff—gone. Where was she? Stunned, he turned and walked back to Josie, who still stood by the table where he had left her. "Where is she?"

"She made me promise not to tell you." Tears welled in her eyes. "She was really upset. What happened with you two?"

"Nothing," he said.

"Something had to have. She's gone."

He shook his head. He didn't know. "Where did she go, Josie? Tell me."

"I can't break my promise." She sank down in a chair and fiddled with a blank envelope. "I hate being put in the middle of this."

He couldn't believe it; she wasn't going to help him. He would have to find Lorelei on his own.

"I can tell you her car left thirty minutes ago."

"She left a half hour ago?" He looked at his watch. "She

hates driving in the snow. Where was she heading?"

"I can't tell you that."

"But you just told me she left thirty minutes ago."

"No. I said *her car* left."

He raked his hands through his hair. This was a game of semantics. He hadn't the patience for it. Time was wasting. He took a deep breath. "Was *her car* headed toward Grayling or Mancelona?" he said through gritted teeth, barely holding on to his temper.

"Grayling."

The highway! "Was *her car* heading south from there?"

"No. North."

"North!" He threw up his hands. "Why would she go north? I would think she would head toward warmer weather."

Josie stood there stricken, nodding her head.

North, north. What was north that would interest her? Mackinac! But the island's season was over. But there was Mackinaw City, and she had wanted to go across the bridge to—St. Ignace! That's where she was headed. "I'm going after her."

"Her *car* doesn't like snow and goes slow."

He could see the worry for Lorelei etched on Josie's face. "I know. I'll find her." He turned to leave.

"Oh, Garth—"

He stopped.

She stared at the envelope she had been fidgeting with, though she had turned it over. His breath caught at the sight of his name on it in Lorelei's neat script. He reached for the envelope, but Josie would not release it.

"I'm not supposed to give this to you until tomorrow," she said, still looking at the envelope.

He wanted to give her a good shake. His patience had run out. He could yank it from her hands so she didn't have to break her word. Instead he looked directly into her eyes and gave her a half smile. "It's tomorrow somewhere in the world," he said quietly. He could play word games, too.

Much to his relief she released the envelope—though he wasn't sure if he wanted to open it. It held something other than paper. Something small but bulky.

He slid his finger under the seal. He could feel his heart pounding in his throat as a sense of dread overcame him. He pulled out a folded slip of paper and dropped the rest of the contents into his hand. He squeezed his eyes to shut out the vision of Lorelei's engagement ring then closed his fingers around the diamond band, pressing it into his palm.

Suddenly he realized more than physical pain had caused her tears yesterday. But what was wrong? Obviously something serious.

"I'm sorry, Garth," Josie said, touching his arm lightly. He opened his eyes to see compassion in her warm brown eyes. "She didn't tell me anything. Maybe her letter will explain her reason."

He unfolded the paper cautiously, knowing what he would find. She was saying good-bye—it was the only explanation for the ring—but at least he would know why.

Garth, it read. No endearment, just Garth. He took a calming breath.

> *As you can see I'm returning your ring. Things just won't work out with us. I knew almost from the start but fooled myself into thinking they could. I should have stopped this relationship before it began. I'm not the right person for you. I am so very sorry for hurting you. I hope someday, in your heart, you can forgive me. Lorelei.*

He folded the note. *This isn't right. There has to be more.* He slipped the ring on his little finger as far as it would go, then put on his gloves. Picking up the gift for his niece, he walked out.

❧

How long, Lord? How long am I to be stuck on the side of the road before someone comes along to help me? I admit it was crazy to drive off in the snow. Even more crazy to slide off the road into a ditch.

She watched the large fluffy flakes blanketing her car. Who would be foolish enough to be out in this storm—other than her? No one. Would she freeze to death out here? She rested her head against the steering wheel. *Lord, I was foolish. Please send help.*

She heard a car engine approach and stop on the road. She glanced upward. *Thank You.* She tried to open the car door, but it wouldn't budge. Pushing harder, she almost fell out of the car when the handle was yanked from her grasp. Strong arms caught her from hitting the snow. She looked up into Garth's concerned face.

No, not Garth, anyone but him!

"Are you all right? You're not hurt, are you?" He set her back in her seat and pushed her hair back, searching her face.

"I'm fine, just a little cold."

He wrapped her in his strong arms and held her tight. "When I saw your car in the ditch, I was so afraid you were hurt or worse."

"I'm fine, really. I was going slow. I only slid off the road." She did not push away from him, not wanting to look him in the face.

He scooped her up in his arms. "Let's get you out of the cold."

"I can walk."

"You'll get snow in your shoes," he said as if he were talking to a little child.

A child is just what she felt like, running away from him as she was. Why did he have to be the one to rescue her? How did he find her anyway? By accident, or did Josie tell him?

If Josie had told him more than she was supposed to, he wouldn't be this nice. Maybe he'd been sent to the store for some ice cream or something and just happened—no, that wasn't in this direction.

The driver's door was open. He put her in and reached

across her to turn on the heater full blast. Then he closed the door and went back to her car.

She got a sinking feeling when she had to move her gift for his niece to scoot over to the passenger side. She prayed Josie still had the note. Her heart dropped to her stomach when she noticed a crumpled white paper on the floor of the truck. An envelope.

That didn't mean it held her note to him. But she knew Garth didn't leave trash in his truck. Ever. She reached down and plucked it off the floor. She looked out the windshield to see where he was. He had her purse in his hand and was closing the door.

She unfolded it quickly and caught her breath when she saw Garth's name in her handwriting. She felt the envelope, but the ring was gone. He climbed in and handed her purse to her, glancing at the gift on the seat between them. "I'll come back later to pull your car out. Is there anything else you need right now?"

She dared not look at him. "No."

The ride back to the cottage was painfully silent. She wanted to say something to him, but no words came.

He drove past Josie's driveway and headed for his own. "Where are you taking me?" Even as the question came out, she knew the answer.

"You promised a little girl you would be at her birthday party," he said coolly. "It's a promise I intend to see that you keep."

"I don't think that's a good idea."

"Don't ruin today for her, too. She's so excited about your coming. Every year for the past three years she chose to go skiing, but not this year because you don't ski."

She seemed to have little choice but to go. He put the vehicle in park and took off his gloves. From his left little finger he removed her engagement ring and handed it to her. "Would you wear this?"

"Don't do this, Garth."

"Not for me, for Carie." He extended the ring closer to her. "And my family."

"Garth. . . ," she whispered and swallowed hard.

"Please. . .do it for her." He closed her fingers around it and climbed out.

She felt like a hypocrite slipping the ring back on, but at the same time it was comforting to have it on her finger. He opened her door and handed her the gift, then scooped her up in his arms.

"Please let me walk." This was hard enough without his holding her.

"We're doing it this way. It's what they expect." When he reached the porch he said, "Smile. Remember—we're in love." His words held an edge of bitterness. "At least one of us is."

The birthday girl flung open the door. "She's here!" The excitement in Carie's voice tore at Lori's heart.

"Well, it's about time," Ryan said as Garth set Lori down. "We were beginning to think you two had decided to elope after all."

"He wouldn't dare," Jeannie said.

"Mom would have his hide," Robin said.

"All right, that's enough." Their mother dispersed the group like a hen scattering her chicks.

"Dad," Garth said, "Lorelei's car is stuck in the snow. Could you give me a hand?"

"I'll help," Ryan said.

"May I go, too, Uncle Garth?" Eamon asked.

In less than a minute all the men and even Dustin were getting their coats. There were so many of them that they had to take two vehicles.

She didn't know which was harder, being there with Garth moments earlier or being there now without him. Fortunately Carie monopolized most of her time. Forty-five minutes later the men returned minus Garth. Where was he?

"He'll be along in a few minutes," Garth's dad said. "He wanted to take your CD player inside out of the cold and tell

Josie he pulled your car out of the ditch."

"Thank you," Lori said with a stiff smile. He didn't ask what her car was doing in a ditch on the way to Grayling, but he had to wonder.

Garth returned in time to sing "Happy Birthday" and planted himself at her side with his arm hooked around her waist.

While Carie opened her presents, Garth and Lori stood off to the side. The girl saved Lori's gift for last.

"Oh," she crooned. "It is so beautiful." She jumped up and ran across the room to Lori, hopping over people who were sitting on the floor. "Would you put it on me?" She held out a delicate gold necklace with a crystal heart hanging on it.

Lori clipped it around her neck.

"Thank you, Miss Hayes." She fingered the necklace.

"You're welcome. When I saw it, I knew it was the one for you." Lori was glad she had come and seen the girl's face light up.

Carie looked up to the ceiling and with a mischievous smile put her hand over her mouth to stifle a giggle.

Lori glanced up to where Carie was looking and spied it as Ryan hollered out, "Mistletoe! You have to kiss her, Garth."

Hoots of encouragement came from all corners of the room. No way could Garth bow out gracefully without everyone suspecting something was wrong. How had she missed the mistletoe yesterday? Everyone must have been too busy to notice it.

"A kiss, huh? I'll show you some serious kissing." Garth wrapped his arms around her, dipping her slightly. She held on to him tightly—which was evidently his plan. He captured her lips with his, lingering longer than necessary to appease the crowd of onlookers. Before he brought her back up, she saw the flicker of pain and pleading in his eyes and thought her heart would break.

She was relieved when twenty minutes later Garth announced he would take her home because Josie was expecting her.

eighteen

Garth pulled up to the garage at the top of the hill, cut the engine, and dropped his head on his hands. His head rocked back and forth. "That is the hardest thing I've ever done. I felt like such a fraud, lying to my family that way."

She had felt like a fraud, too, and a dozen other names she had called herself over the past couple hours. He had acted so calm and natural, as if nothing were wrong. If she didn't know better, she would never have guessed there was a problem. She struggled to keep her tears at bay.

Staring at the ring, she knew what she needed to do and slipped it off her finger. "Here." She held it out to him.

His head turned far enough to see the ring, but he made no effort to take it.

"Please take it." She was uncomfortable with him glaring at the ring.

"I don't want it," he said in an even tone and turned his head back down.

Lori placed it on the dashboard with a shaky hand. "It's right there," she said in an equally shaky voice. "I'm sorry." She bit her bottom lip to stop its quivering and reached for the door.

He grabbed her wrist to halt her escape. After a moment's hesitation he said, "Not even an explanation?"

"My note said—"

"That was not an explanation. It was a cop-out." His voice was hard. She felt him shift and turn toward her, still holding her wrist as if it were a lifeline. "Why? What did I do wrong?"

"Nothing. Please, Garth, don't ever think it was you. It's me."

"But I love you so much."

"It won't work. You're better off without me." She freed

herself from his grip.

"I've been in love with you for ten years. I couldn't believe it when you were at Shawn's party with Josie. I had given you up to the Lord—again—for His will to be done. And there you were like a vision. I thought I was dreaming. After all that, I can't let you walk out of my life again. Not without some sort of reason that makes sense."

Drastic measures were called for, or he wouldn't let go. She swallowed hard. "I—I don't love you." The lie hurt her as much as she knew it would hurt him. But it had to be done. She had to let him go. And go he would now.

"I don't believe you!" he said through gritted teeth.

Lori turned to him, a bit startled.

The angry look on his face faded, and he caressed away her tear then repeated in a firm but gentle tone, "I don't believe you." He continued to caress her cheek. "Please don't lie to me, Lor. I want to know what this is all about so *we* can work through it and come out stronger on the other side."

She searched his face not knowing what to say.

"I'm a big boy. I can handle the truth."

Maybe he could handle the truth, but could she handle his rejection? If the truth were the only way to free him, then he would have it. She loved him that much. "I can't—I can't—" The words stuck in her throat. She had ignored the truth for so long—could she even say it?

"There is nothing you and I and God can't work out. I know it. I've loved you too long."

She shook her head, trying to stay her tears. "I'm not the same girl you fell in love with all those years ago." The accident had changed everything. The tears came uncontrollably.

"I was smitten by the girl, but I fell in love with the woman you became." Garth reached over to comfort her.

She pushed his arms away. If she let him hold her, the truth would never be told, and it was the only way—she could see that now. The day of reckoning was at hand. The truth would set him free.

She drew strength from knowing he would be better off without her and sucked in a few ragged breaths until she felt she could talk. "The accident," she squeaked out and realized she couldn't talk yet. She took in more calming breaths.

"The accident when you hurt your hip in high school? You won't marry me because of something that happened ten years ago?"

She nodded as she took a final cleansing breath. "Yes, the accident."

"Your injuries don't matter to me. I love you just as you are." There was a hint of hope in his voice. "I've enjoyed carrying you around." He reached out to her.

She held up a hand to stop him. "Don't—please. You don't know how I am. If you want the whole truth, don't stop me."

"I'm listening," he said softly, facing her.

She avoided looking at him and took a deep breath before plunging ahead. "It was a bad accident. My dad was killed instantly. My mother lingered in the hospital between life and death for twelve hours before she lost the battle. The doctors worked on me for seven hours in surgery. They almost lost me twice. I was in a coma for four and a half weeks. They didn't expect me to wake up. I was the proverbial vegetable hooked up to life-support machines."

"I'm sorry. I didn't realize it was that bad." She could hear a strain in his voice.

She held up her hand as she gave her head a tight shake. He said no more.

"It got worse. I woke up." Bitterness etched her voice. "At first I was barely aware I existed. Once they felt I could handle it, they told me about the accident, my parents, the extent of my injuries, and all they had to do to keep me alive. I wanted to die. I wished I had died."

"Don't say that!"

She turned on him. "It's the truth, Garth! I wanted to die when I woke up in the hospital all battered and my parents dead. There was nothing I wanted to live for. You wanted the truth."

His eyes glistened with unshed tears. The truth was not pretty.

He didn't say anymore, but she could see the hurt on his face. Good. Now the final blow, and he would be free. "I had extensive injuries. Besides a serious head wound, a crushed hip, and a broken leg, I had other problems. Massive internal bleeding headed the list of life-threatening problems. They pumped blood into me, a lot of it to keep me alive to operate on. They didn't have enough time to stop the bleeding, so they started removing nonessential organs that were bleeding heavily in order to repair the vital ones. They took one of my kidneys and part of my liver, then did a hysterectomy." She choked on the last word.

"But you're alive. That's what counts."

"Didn't you hear me?" Anger mixed with her pain. "A hysterectomy. I can't have children. They took it all. It is physically impossible. I will *never* have children!" She breathed heavily from her outburst; she had said everything. And from the stunned expression on his face she knew he finally understood. It was time to go. She turned, reaching for the door handle. It blurred, and she fumbled to get hold of it.

His hand settled on her arm. "Lorelei, I love *you*."

"Stop saying that." Didn't he know it only made it harder?

"Why? Can't *you* handle the truth? I do love you. Nothing you have said changes that."

Was he really that dense? "Garth, if we get married and I can't have children, then you can't have children."

"So?" was his soft reply.

His look was sincere, but she knew his heart. He loved children. "Don't look at me as if it doesn't matter. I know you want kids of your own."

He was silent for a long moment. She knew he couldn't deny it. "Yes, honestly, I always thought or hoped to have kids someday. But I have the kids at school and my nieces and neph—"

She cut him off. "That would never be enough. It's not the same."

"No, it's not, but we can work this out. We could adopt."

She shook her head. "You would come to resent me because I couldn't give you your own children."

"I would never resent you."

"Please, Garth. You're better off without my hanging around your neck weighing you down. I won't trap you in a marriage you would one day regret. I can't do that to you."

"So that's it? End of discussion! *Adios! You* have decided!"

She could hear the anger in his voice. The anger would help him let go. "Good-bye."

"No. There is nothing good about this."

She opened the door and stepped out. He didn't stop her this time or say a word.

She expected him to start the engine and drive away in a huff, but he didn't. He watched her as she walked around the front of the vehicle. She knew his eyes were still on her as she started down the steep grade. This was going to be a long walk with him watching. She hoped she wouldn't fall. As quickly as the thought entered her head, her feet shot out from under her. She felt the impact in her hip.

The truck door opened, and Garth was at her side before she could stand on her own. He scooped her up in his arms as he had done so many times and trudged down the hill.

"I can walk," she said, not wanting to be so close.

He gave her a quick pensive glance then fixed his eyes on the decline before him.

Once at the door he set her inside. Before she could retreat he took her hand and kissed her palm. He curled her fingers over the place his lips had touched. A farewell gesture?

The hurt in his clear blue eyes bore through her. Josie came up behind her and put her hand on her shoulder as she watched his retreating form hike back up the hill. Lori wanted to curl up and die. She dissolved in a puddle of tears in Josie's embrace.

❧

Garth didn't know how long he had sat there with his head back against the headrest and his eyes shut when the passenger door opened. His mother slid in, closing the door behind her. He had come back from Lorelei's but wasn't ready to face his family.

"What's up?" he asked her, trying to shake off his own thoughts.

"I came out to talk to you." Her tone was serious.

"About what?" He had been so absorbed in his own problems of the day he had barely noticed anyone else, let alone their needs.

She gave him a look of chagrin. "I'm not old and senile yet, son. I have eyes to see you are in pain."

He gave a tight smile. "I never could hide anything from you. How could you tell?"

"It's in your eyes. There's trouble between you two. You hardly looked at her the whole time she was here. Though you stood close enough and made a grand gesture of that kiss."

"Do you think anyone else noticed?"

"I don't think so, dear. Did you two have a fight?"

"We have now," he said dryly.

"Talk to her, honey."

"I tried. She won't listen."

"Is it serious? Can you work it out?"

"Oh, it's serious all right." He reached inside the front of his coat and pulled the ring out of his shirt pocket.

"That serious?"

"She was running away from me."

"That explains her car in a ditch on the way to Grayling."

He looked at her, puzzled.

"Your father told me. Do you want to talk about it?"

He rubbed his hands over his face. "She can't have children. The accident she was in was worse than I realized." And yet she mustered the courage to forgive the man. "The doctors had to do some radical surgery to save her life. She thinks I don't want her. She's afraid I'll resent her for not being able to have my children."

"Hysterectomy?"

He nodded.

She nodded in understanding. "Children are our future. Our hope."

"But I can be her future. Aren't I enough to be her hope?"

"You may be too much to hope for. She has had so many losses in her life from what you've told me—her parents, her brother, and her aunt, the children she will never have. You may be her last hope. She is protecting herself from rejection."

"But I'm not rejecting her. I love her."

"Garth, dear, this isn't about you or your love for her."

"I say it is." He shoved the ring toward her so she could see he was the injured party. Why was his mother siding with Lorelei? Shouldn't she be on his side?

"I once read a story about a South Seas man who wanted a bride. The going price was two to five cows."

He frowned at his mother. "Cows, Mom?"

"Do you want to hear my story?"

He shrugged then nodded. It couldn't hurt.

She paused. "Now this man was an accomplished bargainer, and because everyone knew the girl he chose was homely he was sure to make a good deal. The girl ran and hid, fearing humiliation. After the man greeted her parents, he promptly offered eight cows. The deal was made, and the two were married. Many people started to comment on how she had grown more beautiful and asked the man how he did it. He said he had loved her for a long time and knew she felt unworthy to be his wife. He bought her for eight cows to show her and everyone else how valuable she was to him. That was what brought about the change in her.

"Like the girl in the story, Lorelei is running, too. Does that make sense?"

"I think so—where can I find eight cows?"

His mother sighed. "You're impossible."

He did understand. Lorelei was unworthy only because she thought she was.

"Is it over? Are you giving up?" she said.

"I don't know what else to do or say. She returned the ring and told me good-bye."

"If you give up this easily, maybe you're not ready for marriage."

Was his mother right? Was he ready for the rigors of marriage? He tried to picture his future without Lorelei. Bleak and lonesome. He couldn't imagine himself with anyone else. He would spend long, lonely nights pining for her and dreaming of how things could have been, should have been. "Why did she wait until now? She had plenty of opportunities to tell me."

"Did you two ever discuss children?"

"No. I just assumed."

"Maybe she wanted to feel normal, whole. You can't imagine the trauma of losing all hope for the future."

"She said that once, about losing everything in the accident— past, present, and future."

"When you proposed, were you sure?"

"Yes."

"For better or for *worse*?"

"Yes, I think so."

" 'I think so'? You are either committed or not. Don't be a seventeen-minute kind of guy."

He gave a half laugh at that. "Gretchen told you about Lon?"

"Over and over. She couldn't believe he only waited seventeen minutes. We women like to know our men are in for the long haul."

He thought about his mother's words. He was ready to take wedding vows for better or for worse, for richer or for poorer, in sickness and in health. But did he understand what that could mean? If the worst happened and they were dirt poor and she became chronically ill, did he want to be the one at her side—forever?

"Mom, I love her so much."

"But you worry if you love her enough."

He sighed. "I want to hold her in my arms and make her pain go away, to give her everything she ever longed for." He dropped his head. "But I can't do that, can I?"

"That's up to God. You have a decision to make. Do you want to live the rest of your life with Lori? Or do you want to live the rest of your life without her?"

He laid his head back against the headrest. He wanted Lorelei and children. It was never a choice he thought he would have to make.

&

That night Lori woke up in a cold sweat. The nightmare again. Only this time Garth was there, in the light. He looked down at her with disgust and wrenched the child from her. "You can't have this." His voice was laced with loathing. Then the black desolation and oppression enveloped her.

She cried into her pillow until the early morning light.

nineteen

"I can't believe you won't even consider adoption," Josie said, incensed. She had been after Lori all day about Garth and the situation.

"It's not like a real family."

"Thanks a lot. Adoptive families are as real as any other family—to be chosen and know you are wanted. Isn't my family real? A real family is people caring for one another. There are so-called *families* I wouldn't want to be a part of. I'm glad for the parents I have. The parents who chose me, wanted me, raised me."

What was she talking about? Why was she so upset about this?

"Don't look at me as if I have a third eye," Josie said. "You had to know I was adopted."

"You? Adopted? But your family is so close."

"The key word is *family*. Maybe not by blood, but certainly by choice. You've never noticed I look nothing like either one of my parents? They have light brown hair; mine is nearly black. They have fair skin; my complexion is olive. My eyes are so dark brown you can hardly see the pupils; theirs are blue and hazel. I'm sure that somewhere in my ancestry is a Greek and possibly a Romanian, but it's not my mother or father. It's someone whose blood runs through my veins, my ancestors, but not my family."

Lori understood what Josie was saying. Family was more than blood, and her family was proof of that.

"As Christians we're adopted," Josie said. "An adopted child has rights and privileges that even natural-born children don't have. God has made adoption special. You could be a wonderful mother to some child who has no more hope, a

170

child who needs to be loved. And a man out there is waiting to share that future with you."

Josie's words pierced her. She was punishing herself, perpetuating herself as a victim. She was tired of being hurt and lonely, longing for what could never be. It was time to get on with her life, to stop feeling sorry for herself and thinking of what she could have. If Garth could still love her. If he could live with—her—defects. She would gladly give it a try. If he were willing. If it wasn't too late.

Lori walked out onto the snow-covered deck and looked toward the trees and shadows that concealed Garth's place. A shiver rolled through her. She retreated to her room and picked up the little photo book Garth had given her. She turned the pages slowly but stopped when she came to the pair of pictures on adjacent pages at the *Somewhere in Time* marker. She focused on the first picture, the one she hadn't known at the time the man had taken. She had been thinking how Garth had manipulated the situation to get a picture of them together. Her internal voice had cautioned her then. *Careful, girl, or you'll lose your heart to him.* But the warning came too late. She had lost her heart to him ten years ago and hadn't even known it.

She looked about the room. Once again all she would be taking from here would be her memories. She closed her eyes. *Thank You, Lord, for giving me these new memories. You know I want more, but I'm determined to be content with what You have given me.*

She opened her Bible to Proverbs and read: "Trust in the Lord with all your heart and lean not on your own understanding; in all your ways acknowledge him, and he will make your paths straight."

Father God, forgive me for not trusting You. I guess I never really have beyond my salvation. I didn't trust You when I forgave Ray Kent. I did it on my own strength and understanding, but You blessed me anyway. Garth deserves someone who can give him everything. If I had trusted You, things might be different.

I should probably go and apologize in person to him, but I can't bring myself to face him. I surrender completely to You. She took a deep breath. *Please bring a wonderful woman into Garth's life.*

❧

Three more days passed with no word from Garth.

"Are you sure you want to leave with me today?" Josie said.

"I think it's best."

"You should at least tell him you're leaving."

"I'm gathering my courage to call. I'd go over there, but I don't think my hip is up to a trek in several feet of snow. It'll be hard enough getting up the driveway to my car. If the phone conversation goes okay, maybe I'll consider staying." If she heard any hope in his voice at all, she would stay. She felt sapped of emotion. She had accepted late in the night that she might have lost Garth for good. And if that were the case, she would cherish the memories with him but was determined to get on with her life. She should call Garth so they could be on their way. She had written him a note in case he refused to talk to her. But first she would finish her tea.

They sat in silence for a while longer clutching their mugs of cold tea. The sudden knock at the door cut through the silence. They both jumped and looked at one another. Josie rose, straightening her robe, and peeked out the window. Lori heard a small, whispered voice; then Josie closed the door, handing a thick envelope to her. *Lorelei* was scrawled on it in Garth's best writing with a little flourish underneath and a small heart in place of the *o* in her name.

She opened the envelope slowly, trying to keep her hopes in check. The note could say anything, like "Sorry, but I think you were right, so long." But the heart—it was a heart of hope.

Just a short note to tell you I'm smiling. I have hope again. I believe with all my heart you are the one for me. I'm trusting God to make it so. I made you a promise of lasting love. I will not go back on it nor my promise of marriage. I will be here when you are ready, even if it takes a lifetime.

He poured out his heart and his dreams of their future: page after page, scenario after scenario, of what their life together could be like. Endless possibilities. Each one ended with "and they lived happily ever after."

I guess this is more than a short note, but once I got started I couldn't stop. You are so easy to talk to. One more thing—I applied for a teaching position on Mackinac Island, and Will thinks I have it clinched—though it isn't official. He's looking for a house for us. Yours truly, now and forever, Garth.

P.S. Look out the window at the lake. A surprise awaits you.

She pulled back the curtain, and her breath caught. A broad path had been shoveled from the beach out a ways onto the ice. The dock that floated in the water by summer rested upon the now-frozen lake. The dock where she had first encountered Garth.

Josie came up beside her and looked out. "What fool would drag a dock out on the ice?" After a moment she said with a smile in her voice, "A fool in love."

Like Ne-Daw-Mist, the Indian maiden on Mackinac Island held captive by her father, Lori had been held captive by her own self-pity, and Garth was her brave of the sky people. Or was he the fairy king of this enchanted lake?

Lord, thank You for a second chance. Thank You for bringing me here. And thank You for Your love and Garth's.

Snow or not, she had to go see him—now. Even if she had to crawl the whole way. "I won't be going with you today."

"Duh."

She gave Josie a quick hug and slipped into her coat. But when she opened the door she stopped short. Garth stood in the breezeway, leaning against the woodbox.

"How did you know?"

"I told you in my letter I'd be here when you were ready." He held out his arms.

She stepped down into the breezeway and into his embrace. "I'm ready."

His gaze captivated her. "Miss Lorelei Hayes, will you marry me?"

She found she had no breath to answer him and nodded.

He leaned forward as if to kiss her then pulled back and handed her a small black-and-white stuffed cow. "The first of many."

"Why are you giving me a cow?"

"Did I ever tell you the story about the South Seas man and the eight cows?"

"No." She blinked several times.

"It can wait until later. I have other plans at the moment." He captured her lips with his.

Who cared about cows? She sighed and leaned into his embrace. She was home.

A Letter To Our Readers

Dear Reader:
In order that we might better contribute to your reading enjoyment, we would appreciate your taking a few minutes to respond to the following questions. We welcome your comments and read each form and letter we receive. When completed, please return to the following:

Fiction Editor
Heartsong Presents
PO Box 719
Uhrichsville, Ohio 44683

1. Did you enjoy reading *Lakeside* by Mary Davis?
   ❑ Very much! I would like to see more books by this author!
   ❑ Moderately. I would have enjoyed it more if

   _____
   _____
   _____

2. Are you a member of **Heartsong Presents**? ❑ Yes ❑ No
   If no, where did you purchase this book? _____
   _____

3. How would you rate, on a scale from 1 (poor) to 5 (superior), the cover design? _____

4. On a scale from 1 (poor) to 10 (superior), please rate the following elements.

   ____ Heroine   ____ Plot
   ____ Hero   ____ Inspirational theme
   ____ Setting   ____ Secondary characters

5. These characters were special because? _____
_____
_____

6. How has this book inspired your life? _____
_____
_____

7. What settings would you like to see covered in future
   Heartsong Presents books? _____
_____
_____

8. What are some inspirational themes you would like to see
   treated in future books? _____
_____
_____

9. Would you be interested in reading other **Heartsong
   Presents** titles? ❏ Yes ❏ No

10. Please check your age range:
   ❏ Under 18   ❏ 18-24
   ❏ 25-34   ❏ 35-45
   ❏ 46-55   ❏ Over 55

Name _____
Occupation _____
Address _____
City, State, Zip _____